I0740954

Table of Contents

Chapter One

Tuesday, 3:30 AM

It was a clear night and still comfortable for the time of year. The were crowds finally calling it a night and heading home. Traffic was slowly waning; mostly cabs cruising for stragglers, and the odd late night hopeful looking to score one of the homeless hippie chicks. Only the after hour night crawlers, and those not lucky enough to have hooked up with a place to crash, still prowled the streets. Most of the clubs were closed, or closing. Even the cops were calling it a day; only one or two patrolmen were still seen walking their beats.

The young, uniformed cop walked casually along the sidewalk on Charles Street W., thinking that so far it has been a good night, not too many drunks, bad trips, fights, or other issues. He glanced quickly into the open alleys as he walked along, looking for any trouble. He was about to walk past yet one more when he thought he heard something in the darkness.

He stopped and looked more intently, placing a hand instinctively on his gun. All he saw at first were several garbage cans against the building and a side door lit by a low watt yellowish light at the far end. He was about to continue on his beat when something moved in the gloom.

"Police," he called, pulling out a flashlight and turning it on.

He cautiously stepped into the alley, his hand still on the gun. Holding the light shoulder high, he took several steps then stopped. There, about twenty feet away, was the body of a man lying on his back, just past the last garbage can. He passed the light over the victim revealing that he had been badly beaten. Bending down, he quickly examined him. He was still alive but unconsciousness. His clothes were torn, and his face a mass of blood.

"Sir? Can you hear me?" he said, with a hand on the man's shoulder gently shaking him.

"Uuuuggghhh," was all he got from the supine figure.

"Okay. You take it easy, I'm going to get help, okay? I'll be right back."

The officer stood up and ran back down the alley to the sidewalk then turned and continued to the call box on the corner. Several minutes later, he was back in the alley. A siren wailed in the distance.

"Help's almost here buddy, so hang on," he said softly.

A moment later, a squad car came to a stop at the end of the alley and a plainclothes cop got out.

"Down here," Officer Jack Connelly, called out.

"Rodriquez. Whatcha got?" the detective asked when he stood behind the cop.

"Looks like someone really kicked the shit outta this guy," the cop said.

"Any ID?"

"Didn't look. Figure'd I'd leave that for you guys," he said, stepping back.

The detective knelt down on a knee and started to check the man. He found a wallet and carefully pulled it out of the man's pants pocket. He flipped it open and checked the contents.

"Hmm. Wasn't a mugging. There's a coupla hundred bucks in here," he muttered to no one in particular. "Shit."

"What?" the young cop asked.

"Huh? Oh, I know this guy. Damn. Okay. You get down to the car and call for the ambulance. We gotta get him to the hospital, quick."

"Yes, sir," the cop said, then headed away.

"Gabe?" Rodriquez said softly, leaning down. "It's me, Manny. Manny Rodriquez. Understand?"

"Uugghh," the man moaned.

"Alright, take it easy, buddy. You jus' lay there okay? You'll be at the hospital real soon."

It was not long before the ambulance arrived and within minutes the paramedics had the man secured on a gurney and were wheeling him into the back of the vehicle.

Rodriquez stood off to the side with a notepad in his hand talking to the young cop who'd discovered the victim.

"Your name?"

"Jack Ross, badge number..." he started to say.

"Yeah, got it," Rodriquez said, pointing at his badge. "So, tell me everything."

Five minutes later, Rodriquez got back in the squad car. Officer Ross stood at the window.

"You did good kid," the detective said. "I'll pass that along to your watch commander. Have a good shift."

"Thanks," Ross said as the car pulled away following the ambulance.

Sargent Gus Ferguson entered the squad room at 7:45, his usual time. He carried a brown paper bag with a toasted onion bagel inside in one hand and a cup of coffee in the other. He was the lead detective on the day shift at the police station covering the Village area over to Queens Park and the University of Toronto campus. He'd served the area for the last fifteen years or more. He walked over to his desk in the corner, put the items on his desk and removed his coat and jacket.

"Mornin'," Manny Rodriquez said, behind him.

"Mornin'," Gus answered, as he sat down and opened the bag. "Busy night?"

"No more than usual," Manny said, pulling a chair over and sitting down. "Did get somethin' you might be interested in."

"Yeah? What?" Gus said, taking out the still warm bagel.

"You know Gabe Herschon, right?"

He nodded. "Uh-huh, why?"

"Looks like he got beat up pretty bad last night, and I mean pretty bad. Beat cop found him around three-thirty this mornin' in an alley down by his club. I caught the call and checked it out. Whoever did this really did a fuckin' number on him, man."

"Is he...?"

"Dead? Naw, but he ain't in a good way though. He was taken over to Mount Sinai, him bein' a Jew an' all. When I left, he was still out. Ain't he a friend of you, Abe, and Murph?"

"Yeah. More Murph than us. They've known each other a long time," Gus said. "Okay, write it up and give it to me."

"You gonna tell him? Murph?" Manny asked, standing up.

"Yeah. I'll call him later."

* * *

Springtime in the Village.

A time of renewal, rebirth, hope. A hallmark of life in the Village...or it used to be. I sometimes find it hard to reconcile all the crap that is going on these days when the world outside looks so...hopeful.

Racial tensions, protests, war. It's not like there isn't enough shit going on in our daily lives already. Makes one wonder what's the point. But then that's the bigger, wider world. Happily, mine is filled with three good things to keep my cynicism at bay: Jane and my two girls.

It was a warm April day, and I was taking advantage of it with my feet up on the windowsill enjoying the cool breeze coming in through the open window. I had just finished another one of those cases that starts out pretty straightforward, but then goes sideways, leaving you thinking how many lives you have left, how much luck is left in the well. At least I didn't get shot this time, I thought, but that didn't mean someone didn't try. I gazed out at the late afternoon, watching the sun slowly creeping up the face of the building across the street from my office.

A few years back an aunt who thought well of me, passed on and left me her house on Spadina Street. She was always a sweetheart and doted on my wife and kids who loved her. It was a modest two-story building with three bedrooms and a convenient space on the main floor for me to set up my business office as the bold black letters next to my front door declared to all and sundry: Murphy Confidential Investigations.

That's me. Matt Murphy, Private Investigator. Still healthy and in reasonably good condition, thanks to a regular workout schedule — sort of. I like to think that I can still turn a head or two among the fairer sex, although Maggie, my girl Friday, just rolls her eyes whenever I mention it. But don't confuse me with your dime novel variety gumshoe peeper. You know the stereotype, tough guy, hard as rock macho dude, a smoke hanging from the corner of a mouth twisted in disdain, straight up whiskey in one hand, and big chested peroxide blondes aching to bed him hanging off his shoulder, while the hard asses eye him with a mix of fear and hate. Nope, that's not me.

I actually do work as a P.I., mostly for a couple of insurance companies, investigating questionable claims and for a small law firm serving papers and such. Best part is, they keep me on retainer, so the cheques come in on a bi-weekly basis. Second best thing is, these cases usually don't put me in anyone's cross hairs, or in any other situation that might result in bodily harm. Although I have taken on the odd case or two that has proved the exception to the rule.

Normally I don't take on cases that require me to carry my gun anymore. I have in the past, and the result was what you might expect. Whenever someone comes through my door with a problem that needs a gun, I remember the face of a young woman from several years ago that I was forced to shoot, and several other situations, including my last case, where I took a hit from a bullet. I usually turn these cases down or refer them to someone else...but not always. I'm a sucker for a good sob story, or if a friend is in need of help.

I continued watching the sun slowly inch its way up the face of the building across the street and took a sip of coffee from the mug I was holding, when Maggie buzzed me saying Gus Ferguson was on the phone. Gus and I go way back.

Before hanging out my shingle, I walked a beat as one the city's finest. Back then there were three of us: Gus Ferguson, Abe Goldman, and me. Some of the older guys used to call us the three musketeers. Anyway, it didn't take me long to discover that I wasn't cut out to a beat cop, not so the other two, especially, Abe. He was born to be a cop. And a good one. He rose quickly through the ranks to become a lieutenant in the detective squad. He'd since moved over to Internal Affairs, while Gus made Detective Sergeant in the serious crime squad. Anyway, the three of us have kept up our friendship over the years.

"Gus," I said, when I picked up the phone.

"Murph," Gus said, in his usual terse way.

"What's up? Am I in trouble?" I said, smiling.

"Not that I know about," he said, his tone easy and friendly. "Thought you should know. Early this morning, Gabe Herschon was found in an alley near his home over on Charles Street West. He was worked over pretty bad."

"Jesus, is he...?" I started to say, dropping my feet to the floor, and sitting up.

"No, but he's in a coma or something. He's over at Mount Sinai."

"You got anything on who or why?"

"Not yet. So far, it looks like a random attack, not a mugging. Seems nothing was taken. Manny caught the case, but it don't look good. You know how these cases work. We'll be lucky to give it thirty-six hours," Gus said.

"Yeah, I know."

"I'm talking to you 'cause of your friendship with Gabe. I figure maybe you could poke around and do what you do best."

"Yeah, thanks, Gus. I appreciate this. I'll look into it, and if I get anything you can use, I'll...," I said.

"Pass it on to Manny, okay? It's his case. I'll give him a head's up," he said, interrupting me.

"Okay. Thanks for the call."

"Yeah, by the way, you talked to Abe lately?"

"Not for a couple of days, why? Something up?"

"Give em a call. He'll fill ya in," he said.

I looked at my watch. I knew he'd be in his office by now.

"Will do an' thanks." I disconnected to call then dialed Abe's direct number.

"Goldman."

"Hey, buddy," I said.

"What's up?"

"Just got off the horn with Gus. Gabe was attacked last night. Apparently, he was messed up pretty bad. He's in Mount Sinai. I'm heading over there after I hang up."

"Mugging?"

"Gus doesn't think so. Looks like nothing was taken."

"Okay, keep me posted on how he's doing, now, why did you really call?"

"Gus kinda said I should talk to you."

"Yeah, okay. I was planning on telling you on the weekend but now's as good a time as any," he said, pausing a moment. "I put my papers in."

"Really?"

"Uh-huh. It's time. I'm ready."

I knew that he had been feeling like the job didn't matter to him anymore. All the years on the street dealing with the bottom of the barrel, then having to deal with bad cops and corruption that had almost cost him his life took its toll. Like he once said, it ate at everything that kept him believing that he made a difference. I guess he finally reached the realization that the plate was empty, and he had nothing left.

"If that's what you want then I'm with you a hundred percent," I said.

"I know, Matt, thanks. Look, can we leave this 'til later? Maybe over lunch at the deli."

"Yeah, no sweat. Want me to keep this under my hat?"

"You mean, tell Jane? No, that's cool. Besides, I suspect Millie's already told her."

Our wives, Millie and Jane, are very close friends.

"Okay. I'll get back to you 'bout lunch. See ya then," I said, then hung up.

I got up and grabbed my hat and jacket.

Gabe Herschon and I have known each other for almost ten years. Gabe was a first-generation Jew from Europe, sent here before the war. He was pushing forty-five but keeps fit and is openly gay.

When I first met him, I was still in uniform and walking the beat in Yorkville – Queen's Park area, that was before it became a hippie haven. Later, when it morphed into a mecca of the counterculture movement and I was a civilian again and single, I used to frequent some of the clubs. The entertainments that followed the movement were great with the likes of Gordon Lightfoot, Ian and Sylvia, and some of the U.S performers that came up from Greenwich Village in New York.

That was how I met Gabe. He was working at the King Cole Room in the Park Plaza Hotel as a waiter. Monique's was one of my favourite clubs because they always had some of the best music. It didn't matter, or bother me, that it was also a popular gay bar. In fact, I once did the owner a good turn soon after I hung out my shingle as a P.I. The word was put out among the patrons that I wasn't on the menu.

I learned Gabe was very well connected in the Village scene, especially within the local art community and proved to be a valuable source of information on a couple of past cases. The only other person I knew who had more information was a character named Crazy Pete. Unfortunately, he's now gone. Killed by some rich kids looking for kicks.

"Everything okay?" Maggie asked, when I entered the outer office.

Maggie Garrett has been my girl Friday for the last four years. She's an intelligent twenty-five-year-old woman with a bright disposition and a great sense of organization. She's also not too hard to look at: five-five, a hundred and fifteen pounds distributed perfectly over her slender body. Don't get me wrong here, there's nothing beyond our working relationship going on. My wife is more than enough for me, besides she's in a relationship with a two-hundred-and-fifty-pound pro-football player.

I shook my head. "No. Gabe was attacked and badly beaten last night."

"Oh no. Is he dead?" she said, her voice heavy with concern. She's known Gabe only a short while but they liked each other. Maggie had met him on several occasions and the two hit it off right from the start. In fact, Gabe took to her and treated her like a kid sister and was protective of her. It was fun to watch sometimes because, for some reason, Maggie was surprisingly comfortable being doted on. She's got a very definite independent streak in her.

"No. He's over at Mount Sinai. I'm headin' over there now to check it out."

"Please call me if you find out anything," she said as I left.

"Okay."

When I arrived at the hospital, I was told that he was still in intensive care. He was stable but still unconscious. They wouldn't let me in to see him, but I had a chance to talk with the duty doctor. According to him, Gabe sustained a very severe beating. He had a concussion, four broken ribs and his face might need surgery to fix his jaw, probably from being kicked, and multiple lacerations around his face. I've seen bad beatings before, but this, this had all the earmarks of a savage, brutal attack intended to kill.

I stood listening to the doctor and getting angrier with each description. I wanted the ones who did this and not just because Gabe was my friend. No one deserved to be brutalized like this. Well, maybe the ones who did it.

After I left the hospital, I decided to walk up to the King Cole to let them know what happened and to calm down and think. Gus said it wasn't a mugging, so that left only two other reasons: a random attack or, a deliberate one. In either case, why single Gabe out.

Again, the only reason I could think of was because of who and what he is – a Jew and gay and, with the recent influx of draft dodgers and deserters from the States, many of them good ole southern boys, this looked most likely to be the case. The Village seemed to have become the northern mecca for the hippie generation and social dissidents, like these escapees from the U.S military.

It has been a while since I walked through the Village. Outwardly, not much seemed to have changed, the old familiar buildings were still there, but just behind the old facades I sensed something was different.

The streets were filled with young people hanging around all the usual clubs and cafes, though now they wore jeans and long hair. Even the music had changed from the usual jazz and folk sounds to a more electric sound. But it was the undercurrent of anger that seemed to be fuelling these changes. Tensions were running high, especially in and around the Village, as protesters and students gathered and marched against the war in Vietnam, and the unrest among blacks as part of the growing Civil Rights

Movement. Not to forget the rising prejudice against the homosexual community.

People were turning away from long held family traditions and blindly accepting the rule of government. Now there was an overt feeling of mistrust and discontent that seemed to be signalling changes to come that would alter our country significantly. I wonder if the country was ready...if I was ready. I turned onto Yorkville Avenue and headed for the club.

Chapter Two

The King Cole Room is one of the older clubs still around with its own unique history. Nowadays, it was one of the Village's more openly and popular gay bars.

I opened the door and went inside. The place was about two thirds full with regulars sitting around discussing or arguing the events of the day. I spotted Maxie in his usual place behind the counter and headed over.

"Kinda figured ya'd be in," he said, placing a cup of coffee down in front of me.

"Thanks. So, I guess everyone knows?" I said, putting my hat on the bar.

"Uh-huh. Cops been in and out a coupla times."

"You able to tell them anything?"

He shook his head. "Naw. Wasn't workin' las' night."

"You got any ideas?"

"Maybe."

"So?"

"My guess was 'cause him being queer, ya know," he said, leaning forward.

"Everyone knew he was gay. He made no secret about it," I said.

"Yeah, 'spose that's true. But lately sum 'crackers' been causin' problems for a lot of guys like Gabe."

"Yeah? Like how?"

"Ya know, runnin' the clubs and hasslin' anyone they figure is queer, least that's what I'm hearin'."

"How do you know it's these 'crackers'?"

"Way I hear it, these guys are from the south, ya know, can't mistake their accents an' all," he said, imitating a southern drawl. "They say they're deserters from the army, or sumthin' like that."

"And they been hassling the local gays?"

"Yeah, and not jus' them."

"Yeah?"

"They been goin' after the kids, ya know, the ones been protestin'. They also been chasin' the skirts too."

"You called them, crackers, how come?"

"'Bout ten years back, I worked a coupla clubs down on the river, ya know, the Ole Miss. Learned firsthand what them guys was like. Pretty sure summa them guys was KKK."

"And you think that's who these guys are?"

Maxie shrugged and said, "Maybe. Sure act and talk like them."

"You tell this to the cops?"

"Uh-huh. Those guys ain't nothin' but garbage an' we don't need them here."

"You say that these guys have been harassing Gabe?"

"Yeah, I think so. But I don't think they was doin' it in the club."

"You know if Gabe been seeing anyone special?"

"Funny you ask. Yeah, I think there was this pretty boy been in and out here lately that caught his eye."

"Got a name?"

He shook his head, "Not really. I think Gabe might've said somethin' like Shawn maybe."

"Got any idea where I can find this guy?"

"Nope. But I think I once heard somethin' about being from over near the Park." He was referring to Queen's Park down by the University of Toronto. The area around the Park was popular with gays.

"Okay, thanks. If you think of anything else call me," I said, passing him aa business card. "You think I can take a look in the office?"

"Yeah, sure. Go on back. Door's not locked."

"Thanks," I said, slipping off the stool and going into the backroom area where a small kitchen prepared a small but tasty menu of items.

I waved at Silvia Bono, the cook, who was busy prepping something for a customer. She had been at the club for over five years.

The office was about the size of a closet. A small table and chair were placed against the wall on the right and small file cabinet was set in a corner. I went and rummaged through the papers on the desk. Mostly bills and receipts for inventory used by the club, not much else. I was about to leave when I spotted something on the floor behind one of the table's legs, a crumpled wad of paper. Must have bounced off the rim of the wastebasket. I picked it up and smoothed it open on the desk. Scrawled in thick black ink block letters under a crude drawing of a hanging man were the words:

'DEATH TO QUEERS AND JEWS'

There was also the Nazi swastika and a stylized SS. I folded it up and put it in my pocket then returned to the club.

"So? Ya goin' ta look inta this?" Maxie asked.

I nodded, "Yeah."

"Good. I like Gabe. He's good people. Don't deserve this kinda crap, don't care if he is queer."

"Yeah, he is," I said. "If something comes to mind you know how to reach me."

"You bet," he said, waving off the dollar bill I offered for the coffee. I left it as a tip.

My next stop was the 6th Precinct and Manny Rodriquez.

I don't visit the old precinct as often anymore, not since Abe Goldman left as head of the Homicide Squad, to take up a new position with Internal Affairs. I still knew quite a few of the old timers like Gus Ferguson and Manny, and luckily, Bill Jenkins, who was presently the duty Desk Sargent.

The precinct's main floor was filled with people, as usual. Mostly citizens with complaints and several uniforms holding cuffed perpetrators waiting to process them. Jenkins was presently fending off a couple of Public Defenders trying to get in to see their clients.

Funny how crime always seemed to be a growth industry.

When I finally got Bill's attention, I waved and pointed upstairs. He waved back and nodded okay.

As it turned out, I arrived just about the time for the shift change. I knew Manny would be in because, for some reason, he always preferred the night shift.

Gus was sitting in his usual corner at a desk with stacks of folders and papers covering it.

"Hey," I said, pulling a chair over and sitting down. "Things look 'bout the same."

"Murph. Yeah, same ole shit just piled higher. Guess you're here because of Gabe?"

"Yeah. Thought I'd have chat with Manny before he headed home."

"Okay. He's in the john, should back in a bit. You have a look around yet?"

I nodded. "Uh-huh. Stopped by the hospital first. He's still in intensive care and unconscious, at least as of an hour ago. Then

I stopped at the club. Had a chat with Maxie, you remember him. Poked around the office and found this on the floor behind the table.”

I pulled out the piece of paper and held it out to him by a corner.

“Don't know if the lab boys can get anything from it but it's yours.”

Gus took the page and unfolded it. His expression didn't change as he read the words.

“You don't look surprised,” I said.

“Not really. We've been gettin' a lot of this shit lately.”

“Really?”

“Uh-huh, not just this kinda crap but a lot of shit. Civil Rights protests. Anti friggin' war protests. Women's lib, Christ, you name it. It's like the ship's sinkin,” he sounded tired, or maybe even a bit defeated, “an’ all the lifeboats are leakin’.”

“I know things are getting really crazy out there, but I haven't been hearing anything about it getting violent. Definitely not like this.”

“Yeah, well, that's changin'. You hear about the black movement down in the States?”

He was referring to the recent protest demonstrations and confrontations between black residents and the authorities.

I shook my head. “No actually. Now we got the girls we tend to stay at home more and I don’t keep up on things like I used to.”

"Yeah, well, probably a good thing. I don't think even your buddy could cover your ass these days," Gus said.

He was talking about a good friend of mine, a black man named Terry Jackson, or simply 'T' to his friends. He had a bit of a shady background from his days back in Harlem. But he left and came here in fifty-seven. He married a local girl, Thelma Sparks. I decided I'd give him a call some time real soon to catch up.

"There's Manny," Gus said, nodding toward the door.

"Okay, thanks. Keep the faith," I said, standing up.

"Now where did I put that brochure on available chicken farms?," he said, sarcastically, going through the motions of looking for something among the papers on his desk.

"Funny. See ya later."

"Say hi to Jane for me. Here, give this Manny." He passed the sheet of paper I gave him back to me. "Oh, by the way, you talk to Abe?"

"Uh-huh. We're getting together for lunch at 's Mel's on Saturday if you're free." Mel's was a deli the three of us always met at for lunch.

Gus just nodded as I headed over to Manny's desk.

"Wondered when you'd show up." he said when I arrived and sat down.

"Yeah, good to see you too," I said. I passed the sheet of paper to him after he sat down.

"What's this?"

"I was poking around at the club and found this in the office. It was on the floor behind the table. Easy to miss."

He took the page and read it. "So, looks like he might've been targeted."

"Yep. Looks that way. Gus said that it's not as unusual as one might think. That mean there's more of these people up here peddling this crap?" I asked.

"Unfortunately. It's like all the crazies have come outta the woodwork, ya know. I know the Village has had it's share of controversy and stuff, but now it's like it's all gone to hell in a hand basket."

"So, I guess that means you guys got something on these people."

"No, but the boys over at headquarters might. They set up a special unit as part of a FBI initiative to keep track on what's goin' on with these so called radicals and deserters that've been makin' their way north. Christ, they're even sayin' these people are actually Communists agitators, can you believe that?"

"The Bureau? You bet I can. Hoover is crazy about the so-called Red problem. So, you got any contacts over there I can talk to?"

"Yeah. I know one or two of the guys who'll probably talk to ya. I'll make a call, set somethin' up. But don't expect too much cooperation."

"Whaddya mean?"

"The feds are runnin' the show over there an' our guys aren't too crazy 'bout that, so you might get somethin'."

"Okay, thanks."

"I'll call ya if I can set up a meetin'."

"Thanks, Manny. I appreciate this. By the way, you give any thought about why the attack happened?"

"Well it wasn't a muggin'. Only other thing might hafta do with him bein' gay, right? Been hearin' 'bout similar shit happenin' up over round the Park. 'Though nothin' like this."

"That might be closer to the truth than you know. Maxie, at the club, told me that Gabe might be hooked up with some young stud named Shawn. Said he heard that this guy might live over in the Park area."

"That it?"

I nodded, "Uh-huh."

"Thanks. I'll have another talk with Maxie later."

"And if I dig up anything else I'll get it to you."

"Deal. Good luck."

We shook hands as I stood up. Looking over at Gus I waved goodbye then headed for home.

I picked up the evening paper on the way to the subway station. It was only a twenty-minute ride up to where I lived. Most of the news was disheartening. Protests. Confrontations between students and minorities and the police. Casualty lists and reports from Vietnam. With thoughts of Gabe laying unconscious on a hospital bed foremost in my thoughts, I couldn't read all this negative news. I flipped over to the entertainment section and perused the listings of clubs and theatres.

Like I said before, we, my wife Jane and our two daughters, Mary and the baby, Alice, live happily in a comfortable house I inherited. This was my oasis, my sanctuary from the madness of the world. Not a day goes by that I don't wonder at my good luck to have the love of a woman like Jane or the treasures she gave me.

I could smell the aroma of roast chicken emanating from inside as I inserted the key into the lock.

"Daddy," squealed Mary, as I stepped inside, closing the door behind me.

She flew off the couch where she was sitting watching the television and charged at me, arms held out. This was our daily routine when I came home. A highlight of my day.

"Hi, baby," I said, scooping her up as she wrapped her arms around my neck.

She was the spitting image of her mother. Same hair. Same eyes. Same amazing smile. I look at her and know that before long I'd be dealing with a parade of boys. When I thought of that time, I got a knot in my gut. Jane always laughed whenever I said anything about it, re-assuring me that we had nothing to worry about.

"Hello, sweetheart," Jane called from the kitchen. "Dinner will be ready in ten minutes."

"Okay," I called back, peeling my daughter away and setting her on the floor.

Jane came out of the kitchen a moment later and over to me.

"That's enough sweetie," she said to Mary, "it's Mommy's turn."

"'Kay," the little girl said as she dashed back to the couch.

Jane wrapped her arms around my chest and gave me a soft, warm kiss on the lips, then stepped back and looked into my eyes.

"What's wrong? Something happen?" she asked, looking at intently at me.

Amazing, I thought, smiling. She always knew when something was on my mind even as far back as when we first met.

"Yeah. It's Gabe," I asked as I remove my jacket.

"Oh God. What happened?" She knew Gabe, and they were good friends.

"He got jumped last night and got beaten up pretty bad."

"Oh no. Was it a mugging?" she asked, sitting on the arm of the sofa chair.

"Don't look that way. In fact, it looks like it was a targeted attack because he's gay and a Jew."

"How awful. Is he okay?"

I shook my head. "Not really. He in Mount Sinai. I stopped in to check on him, he's still unconscious. The beating was really savage the doctor said he's got a cracked skull and a couple busted ribs."

"What about the police? They got anything?"

"I stopped in and had a talk with Gus and Manny. So far, they haven't got a thing. Gus asked if I'd poke around because of my connection with Gabe."

She looked up at me and smiled. "I imagine he didn't really need to ask, did he?"

"No," I said.

"Well, just be careful," she said, softly.

Chapter Three

I arrived at the office at eleven. I had stopped at the hospital for a quick update. No change. Maggie was at her usual place behind her desk. She usually beat me in and always had a fresh pot of coffee ready. It was time to re-visit the Village; get re-acquainted with old contacts and updated on what was happening. I still had people and places I could go to even though I'd been out of touch for a year or so. Suddenly, Crazy Pete came to mind.

Crazy Pete. A well-known fixture of the Village. To many, he was thought of as just a 'local character'. He always dressed in mismatched flamboyantly coloured clothes and long pointy shoes. Those in the know, knew him as a petty thief, hustler, and deadly with a knife. I knew all these things as well but, I also knew that he knew everything that went on in the Village, especially its underbelly, its darker side. But he was gone now; killed a couple years back by some college kids over a game of pool.

I checked my watch: eleven-fifteen. I picked up the phone and dialed.

"Ed's," said a gruff sounding voice through the earpiece.

"Hi, Ed. It's me, Murph," I said.

"Jesus, man. Long time no hear. How'ya doing?"

"Yeah, it's been a while."

"So? What's up?"

"You got some time to talk?"

"For you, anytime," he said. "I ain't forgot what ya did for Pete."

"Thanks. In a couple of hours, okay?"

"Works for me. Care ta give a hint?"

"Looking to get caught up on what's happening around the Village."

"Guess family life takes up a lotta yer time, eh?"

"Uh-huh. See you soon," I said, then hung up.

A moment later Maggie buzzed me that Manny Rodriquez was on the line.

"Hey," I said, when I picked up the phone.

"I got a name for you. I spoke to him and he's willin' to talk to you. His name is Art Holman. A detective with that special squad workin' with the Bureau. He's a good guy. Old school, if ya get me."

"Yeah I do, thanks, Manny," I said.

"No sweat. By the way, you get anything yet?"

"No. I'm going to start talking to some people I know, see what's I can find out."

"Okay, keep me updated, okay?"

"You'll be the first one I call."

He gave me a phone number for Holman then hung up.

I decided I would call Holman later. Right now, what I needed was any information on these Southerners and that meant talking to Ed and others. People who would talk to me, maybe, before ever talking to the cops. Besides, if Holman talked to me and gave up anything useful he would expect a quid pro quo from me. I don't have a problem sharing with the police as a rule, but I'd have to be careful here because of the feds. They didn't play by the same rules, or as nice.

I got up and put on my jacket and hat.

"Heading out?" Maggie asked, when I stepped out of my office.

"Uh-huh. I'll be gone most of the day, but I'll check in," I said, giving her Holman's number. "Here, give this guy a call and see if you can set up a meeting with him. Tell him anytime is good for me. I'll call in later see what you got."

"Are you going to hospital by any chance?" she asked, taking the piece of paper with the phone number on it.

I nodded. "Uh-huh."

She smiled. "If he's awake, tell him I said hi and I'll be by later, okay?"

"Will do."

Once outside, I flagged a cab and headed for Ed's.

Every neighbourhood in almost every city has a set of permanent fixtures: mom and pop stops, delicatessens, bars, and pool halls. Places where the local denizens meet to exchange gossip and argue the news of the day. Ed's Bar and Pool Hall was a little different. His 'clientele' were hustlers, bookies, and other shady characters. Then again, maybe not so different than any other pool hall.

I stepped inside and it felt like I had stepped back in time. Nothing had changed. It was as dark as usual. The air was thick with the odor of stale smoke, booze, and the talcum powder used to keep cues smooth. Same bar, same stools. Same pool tables with the same men eyeing anyone who came in with suspicious looks, sitting around watching pigeons getting fleeced.

"Jesus H. Christ, Murph. How da fuck are ya?" Ed said, from his usual spot at the end of the bar at the back.

Ed McCain has owned this place forever. He once told me he inherited it from his old man. Ed was in his mid to late sixties, white haired and showing most of those years on his face. He was also overweight with a substantial beer belly.

He was well connected in the neighbourhood and, I suspect, in a couple of other 'quarters' not completely kosher. Many of the local area lowlifes passed through his place. I think it's because his place was accepted as neutral ground.

I took a seat on the last stool across from him, glancing quickly at the corner to my right where Pete always sat, his cue stick leaning in the corner. He used to call this place his office.

"Good, Ed, you?" I said.

"Ya know, same ole shit," he said, "coffee, or sumthin' stronger?"

"Coffee, thanks." I took a stool. "See you've still got Pete's cue in place."

"Yeah. Didn't see any point in taking it away. Helps me remember," he said, putting a mug in front of me.

"Thanks."

"So? What brings ya here?"

"The usual. Looking for information," I said, taking a sip of lukewarm coffee. One thing hadn't changed: the coffee. It was still the worst coffee I've ever had.

"No problem. Whatever ya need. Whatcha inta this time?"

I gave him the Reader's Digest version of what happened.

"Jesus. Man, things are goin' in the toilet and startin' ta circle the drain."

"Yeah, seems like it. Anyway, what I need is to get a handle on these assholes. You got anything?"

"Way I hear it, a bunch of these guys, a dozen or so, come up from Tennessee or Kentucky, or one a dem states down south, a while back looking for some trouble. I think they're deserters or them draft dodgers I been readin' about."

"Whaddya mean, 'trouble'?"

"Ya know, stirrin' up all kinds of shit with the blacks and Jews and the fags. Anyway, word on da street is they've been tryin' to recruit members."

"What about violence? Hear anything about them attacking anybody?"

"Yeah, summa da guys come in here tell me that they been seen roamin' da streets at night hasslin' people, if ya get my drift," Ed said, "If you goin' after them better watch yer ass. These guys are 'spose ta be bad asses."

"Count on it. Look, can you nose around and get me as much as you can on these guys, you know, names, addresses, the usual."

"No sweat. You can always come to me, Murph. Anytime. Anything."

"Thanks."

I slid off the stool and, after a quick look at the empty corner with the cue, "Nice touch," I said, looking back at him with a smile.

He shrugged and made a sad smile back. "He was my friend."

"Yeah," I said, "me too. See ya." I headed back outside.

I told the cab driver to take me back to Mount Sinai. Time for another check up on Gabe. On the ride over, I considered what Ed had said, trying to get my head around these guys, and why they were here in the Village. What were they hoping to achieve? The Village had always been one of the most tolerant, accepting places I knew.

I looked out the window at the passing streets and old familiar buildings. I couldn't help feeling that everything I knew and loved about this place was changing into something I wouldn't know anymore, or like. Things seemed to be getting crazier than usual, even for the Village and worse, money was taking an interest in the area and that meant the end of what made it a great place for everyone.

The cab pulled up to the entrance of the hospital and I got out. I checked with the main desk and was informed that Gabe was off the critical list and moved out of intensive care to a regular room. His condition was still listed as serious.

His room was on the second floor. I went to the nurse's station to get his room number in time to meet the duty doctor who just happened to be there.

"You a family member of Mr. Herschon?" he asked when he heard me ask the nurse for the room number.

"No. A friend. Far as I know, he has no immediate family here," I said, shaking the doctor's hand.

"I see. How long have you known him?"

"A long time. Maybe fifteen years, or so," I said.

"Can you tell me if he has any medical history or conditions?"

"None I know about. He was always pretty healthy looking to me, in spite of being soft, a bit on the heavy side, and his smoking.

I guess the only thing I'd say that might matter is that he's gay. I think that's why he was attacked, that and maybe, because he's Jewish."

"Are you a cop?"

"No, but I am a private detective, why do you ask?"

"Nothing, it was just the way you said what you did. Had that cop tone, you know. I take it that your interest may be more than just how your friend is doing."

"You could say that, yeah. So, is he awake yet?"

"He's been slipping in and out. We managed to ease the pressure on his brain so that helped bring him back. He's on a strong cocktail of medications to control the pain and reduce the risk of infections."

"When will I be able to see him?"

The doctor glanced at the chart in his hand then said, "If everything keeps going the way it is, then maybe in a day or two."

"That's great doc, thanks. Here are my contact numbers. Call me if there is any change, will you?" I pulled out a business card and wrote my home number on the back.

"Okay. Give it to the nurse there and she'll put it in the file."

"Thanks, again," I said, shaking his hand again and then passed the card to the nurse behind the desk.

A half hour later I was back in the office.

"What's the latest with Gabe? How is he?" Maggie asked as I stepped through the door.

I nodded, "Yeah, just came from there. He's out of intensive care but still in bad shape. Doctor says he's doing well under the circumstances. We should be able to see him in a couple of days. I left my number. He said they'll call if anything changes."

"Does he have anyone to take care of him when he leaves?" she asked.

It never occurred to me to think about that. Gabe always lived alone. I'm sure there were a few people in his private life, but whether these would be available to care for him I didn't know.

"I don't know. Funny what we discover we really don't know about the people in our lives," I said.

"Is there anything we can do?"

"I'll think about it, maybe I can work something out. But for now, you got anything for me?"

"Not right now. I take it you're going after the people who did this right?"

"Uh-huh," I said.

"Thought as much," Maggie said. "You have any idea who was behind it yet?"

"Looks like some ass holes up from the south somewhere."

"Oh dear. I've read about some of the things those people have done. It isn't good, Matt. By all accounts these are very bad and dangerous people. Why have they come this far north, do you think?”

“Don't know. Maybe it's all these protests and stuff. It's fertile ground to spread their brand of poison, I suppose. Anyway, I need you to find out everything you can on these supremacists. Check with your contacts at the paper. Call Jane at the library as well, see what she can dig up.”

“Okay. What're you going to do?”

“The usual, hit the streets, see if any of the clubs been having any similar problems.”

“Okay.”

“I'll check in periodically.”

“What if Ben calls with something?”

Ben Franklyn was my contact at the insurance company I do work for, and who pays my retainer.

“Take the information and I'll deal with it later.”

“You taking off now?”

I shook my head, “Got to make a call first.”

I went in my office and sat down at my desk. I picked up the phone and dialed.

“T's” said a sultry voice into my ear. The voice belonged to one of Thelma Jackson's waitresses named, Vivian. Thelma always had an eye for hiring only the sexiest and prettiest young black women for the restaurant. I asked her if Elmore was available and waited while she went off to find him.

Thelma was married to one of my closer friends, Elmore Jackson. A one-time hood connected with a black mob run by his life-long friend, Leroy 'Mojo' Johnson back in Harlem. He more or less eased himself into his idea of retirement a few years back but was still connected to that part of his life through Mojo.

Jackson came to Toronto from Harlem about ten or twelve years back. The way he tells it, he decided to make the move north for health reasons. Knowing what he did and who for, it didn't take a long stretch of the imagination to get the drift of what he referred to as, 'health'. He didn't elaborate and I didn't ask.

He and Thelma opened their restaurant, T's, soon after they arrived in Toronto. She specialized in authentic Soul food and Cajun cuisine which she exceled at. It had grown to become very popular with the black community and downtown diners. Jane and I made a point of eating there at least once a month. This of course led to her and Thelma becoming very good friends. T, as she likes to be called by her friends, has more or less taken her under her wing, treating her a younger sister.

Anyway, four white guys sitting at a table took exception to him messing with a white women. They waited until Elmore went to the can then followed him in. I slipped off my stool and went in behind them. I arrived just in time to see two of them holding him while one of the others started to put the fists to him; that was when I stepped in. Five minutes later we exited the washroom, leaving the four men laying on the tiled floor in various stages of consciousness, and thus was born an endearing friendship.

Elmore and I have worked a few cases together over the years. There's no one I trust more to watch my back in a pinch than him; the only other man is Abe.

"Hey sweetness," I said with a smile when Elmore's wife came on the line.

"Murph? Damn, sugar, where y'all been?" Thelma said, sweetly.

"You know, not as loose anymore since becoming a solid citizen," I said.

"Ain't it a bitch when dat happens," she said with a chuckle. "S'ppose y'all want my ole man?"

"If he's up, yeah."

"Funny. Y'all know him, for sure. Jus' a sec," she said.

A moment later Elmore was on the line.

"Whazzup, ma man?"

"You going to be around later today?" I asked, dropping the pleasantries.

"When?"

I glanced at my watch. "Say in a coupla hours?"

"Cool, see ya when ya git here," he said, then hung up.

That's my man. Big time conversationalist. No wasted time or energy. But make no mistake, or think, that means he's slow. I suspect that there are bodies in the ground somewhere who made that mistake.

Abe told me once quite a while back that Jackson was suspected in a couple of unsolved killings back in the States. That may be the case, but until evidence comes to light proving that I will continue to be his friend. Hell, I'd still be his friend even if he was arrested and convicted. These days Elmore was mainly occupied running the restaurant with Thelma.

I arrived at the restaurant around two o'clock. The cab dropped me at the entrance of the alley that led to the receiving door at the end. When I reached it, I opened it and went inside.

Standing over one of two large stoves was the main reason for its success: Rufus 'Jumbo' Jones. He looked to be in his early forties, bald with big brown eyes. He was also about three-hundred-pounds which he carried comfortably enough on a six-foot-six-inch frame. Definitely liked his own cooking.

There were a couple of other young black men in the kitchen dressed in white working over prep tables. One of them gave me the eye. He had an angry look about him. He didn't know me.

"Well now, lookie 'ere, iff'n it ain't our favorite honkie," Jumbo said, with a chuckle, when he saw me. "How y'all doin', my man?"

"Same old," I said, smiling as we slapped hands. "Smells good."

"Bet yer ass it do," he said. "How come we ain't seen y'all and that honey of yours?"

"Kids."

He just nodded in a knowing way as if that explained everything – which of course it did.

"He in his office?" I asked.

"Where else he be."

I headed for the swinging doors that led into the main eating area. There wasn't any trade yet; they only opened for the dinner traffic.

It was a well-appointed room with about fourteen tables that sat four comfortably. There were three booths along one wall with old fashioned red vinyl covered seating. These were for their special customers...like me. In one corner they built a small stage where they brought in some very good talent on Friday and Saturday nights.

"Thanks," I said.

"Doin' Cajun catfish wit dirty rice an' fried okra dis Saturday," he said, behind me.

"Keep it in mind," I called over my shoulder. I'd have to talk to Jane about getting a sitter. Jumbo's catfish was outta this world.

Elmore was sitting in his office bent over an open ledger and a stack of papers. His so called 'office' was a booth next to the small, raised stage facing an open dance floor. T's can handle around eighty to ninety

45

customers on a good night, which is most nights.

"I don't think I'll ever get used to seeing you looking like a regular businessman, man," I said, sliding into an empty chair in front of his desk.

He dropped the pencil he was holding and sat back, looking at me.

"Me neither," he said, with a straight face. "T usually do this."

"Speaking of which, where is she? I didn't see her when I came in." It's not too often Thelma isn't in the restaurant. She a very hands on owner.

"Had a meeting with da lawyers."

"Trouble?"

He shook his head.

"Business. Coffee?"

"Okay, thanks," I said.

"Yo, Jolene. Two joes," he called over to one of the waitresses.

"'Kay," she called back in a sweet-sounding voice.

"So? Whazzup?"

"You remember Gabe Herschon? Down at King Cole's."

"Queer dude? Yeah, so?"

"He got jumped yesterday morning leaving the club. Took a major shit kicking. He's in Mount Sinai in really rough shape. Anyway, cops tell me it doesn't look like a mugging. Nothing appeared to be taken."

"So, he messed with da wrong dude," Jackson said.

"No, it don't look like that either. Besides, Gabe isn't a cruiser, and he isn't into the rough trade. No, this looks like it was a targeted assault, probably by a gang of southern boys, maybe Klan. Word is a bunch of them have come up and been raising shit around the area."

Jolene arrived with two mugs of fresh coffee and set them on the table. I watched with pleasure as she walked away.

"Yeah. I been hearin' summa these muthafuckers been hasslin' the brothers and sisters. Heard they down in the Park to, an' over in da Village. Been hasslin' Village folk, mostly queers and long hairs," he said, bringing me back to the matter at hand.

"You been having any trouble with them?"

"Not fuckin' likely. They ain't that stupid."

I knew what he was saying. They come looking for trouble here they leave in an ambulance, or a hearse, that is if the bodies were ever found.

"You're originally from down south, right? You know anything about these people? I know only what I read about."

"Yeah, I knows 'bout them." He got an angry far-off look into his eyes for a moment. "Ya can't be black from the south an' not know. A lotta bad history."

"Uh-huh, I got that from what I've read about. What I don't get is why they suddenly think they can come up here and peddle their shit."

"Y'all think that this place any different?" he asked.

"Well, yeah. I mean, nobody's chasing you down the streets with guns or cars for Christ's sake. Nobody's shooting you or hanging you from the nearest lamp post for talking to a white woman or keeping you out of anywhere."

"Yeah, we got's the good life sho'nuff," he said sarcastically.

"Screw that, you know what I'm talking about, El. I mean, look at you. You own a very successful Goddamn business which is patronized by a lotta white people as well as blacks, so chill out."

"Ain't what I'm sayin', man. Jus' that we ain't the same as you. What we get, we get on our own, in spite of y'all."

"Yeah, I get that," I said. "I know it isn't the same for you and me but it sure as shit isn't as bad as where you came from."

"Hey, man, bad is bad anywhere. 'Cuz they don't hang a brother don't mean they don't try an' beat us down."

"Yeah, I know, but...aw hell."

I have known him a long time and I usually don't see this side of him. Here was a man that lived most of his life on the wrong side of the law and yet wasn't completely bad. In fact, despite once being a criminal, he had a certain code he lived by. There was a line he set for himself that he wouldn't cross.

I often suspected there was something that gnawed at him, buried deep inside, something that made him the man he became and made him take the road he did. I have never questioned it, opting to just accept the friendship. Color has never been an issue between us.

"'Nuff 'bout politics. You gettin' ready to do your shiny knight thing agin?"

He was referring to time a few years back when Abe was almost killed by a couple of dirty cops, and I went after them and took them down.

"Probably."

"Thought so. Ain't ya gettin' old for that shit? 'Sides, y'all a daddy now, yeah?"

"I know, but he's a friend and I can't let it slide. It isn't in me."

He shook his head. "Guess that's what makes y'all different than the rest. You still carry? 'Cuz if you take a run at these muthas you gonna need to."

"Yeah. I'm still licensed," I said, my throat feeling tight at the thought that I might be going into a shooting situation again settled in.

He sat looking at me for a moment.

"I'm in. If ya need me drop a dime."

"Thanks, El." I stood up. "Okay to use the phone before I take off?"

He nodded and I went over, picked up the phone and dialed.

"It's me, got anything?" I said, when Maggie picked up.

"Yeah. First, the hospital called. Gabe's awake and doing better. I'm going there after I close up."

"That's good news. What else?"

"That detective you told me to call has agreed to meet you. He says he can see you at five o'clock."

"Great. Where?" She gave the name of a bar down by Queen's Park. I knew the place. "Anything else?"

"Uh-huh. I called Jane like you said and she's putting something together for you. Said she'll give it to you tonight."

"Thanks, baby. Look, lock up and take off. I'm out for the rest of the day. If you see Gabe before I do tell him I'll be by, okay?"

"You bet. Be careful," she said, then hung up.

I put the phone back and headed for the door.

"Say hi to T for me, will ya? Let her know we might try and make it up here on Saturday," I said over my shoulder to Elmore, who had buried himself back into his bookwork.

"Got sweet act booked for da weekend you an' your bit 'a sugar'll really dig."

"Already planning on getting a sitter. Jumbo told me 'bout the catfish."

He raised a hand and tossed a quick wave.

"Later."

Chapter Four

Queen's Park is one of Toronto's better known urban parks and one of my favourite places to go with my family, especially on weekends when the weather is good. Jane and I like to pack a picnic lunch and take the kids for a day's outing. Sometimes we're entertained by young musicians who frequent the park for an impromptu jam session. Mary, my oldest, likes listening to the music.

I like coming here sometimes to just sit and think while watching the parade of hippies, old beats, and students, who seem to make up the majority of the population during the weekdays. Over the years I have made a number of contacts, and a few friends, among the locals of the area.

I picked up a chilled Coke and a tuna salad sandwich from a nearby deli, found an empty bench, and parked my butt. I kept an eye open for anyone I knew. Hopefully, I would connect with someone who could give me an update on what was happening.

I didn't have to wait long.

Her name was Rachel Harmon. She owned a small bookshop, selling gay literature among other things. She'd been here since the fifties; one of the last of the old 'Beats' that migrated here from Greenwich Village. She still dressed in black leotards or Capri pants and turtlenecks most of the time. If I had to guess, I'd say she was in her mid to late sixties, but still had a svelte figure and great legs.

I didn't see her when I arrived, so I was a little surprised when I spotted her walking toward me then sit down at the other end of the bench.

"Hey, Murph. How ya doin', man?" she said.

"Rach, hi," I said, smiling. "Didn't see you when I came in."

"Call of nature. So, what brings you here? It isn't the weekend last I looked."

"Lunch," I said, raising the last bit of my snack.

"Right, and...?"

"Working on something. You know Gabe Herschon?"

"Heard the name. Works at King Cole's, right?"

"Uh-huh. He got beaten pretty bad a couple of nights back. Cops don't think it was a mugging. Looks more like a targeted attack."

"Because he's a Jew and gay?"

She knew him alright. She knew almost everybody who'd been around the Village for any length of time. I suspect that she also knew him because she was Jewish and gay like him.

"So, you know him?" I asked, finishing off the last of the sandwich.

"Yeah, I know him," she answered, nodding. "He's well known in the community."

By community, she was referring to the gay community which was fairly large in this area.

"You know if he was involved with anyone serious, or seeing anyone on a regular basis?"

She shook her head. "Not his style. He liked short term hook ups. Word is he's been having a thing with a young stud, Shawn something or other. You know the type, young, beautiful...broke."

"Kinda risky going that route, isn't it?"

"Uh-huh, but, like the saying goes, 'ain't no fool like an old fool', especially an aging queer. By the way, how bad was it? The attack?"

"Pretty bad. A skull fracture and a couple of cracked ribs. But he's awake now and out of intensive care. He's over at Sinai," I said.

"Motherfuckers," she spat. "You got any ideas who or why?"

"Yeah. Like I said, according to the cops, it wasn't a mugging. I been hearing that some redneck types have come up from somewhere down south stirring up trouble. This sounds like it might be them."

"I heard there were some Klan assholes prowling the Village spreadin' their garbage about race purity and keepin' America white. Jesus, can you imagine peddlin' that shit here."

"You hear of anyone being attacked or physically threatened by them?"

"Just the usual shit, hasslin' anybody different, you know, gays, blacks, and some of these youngsters coming into the Village lately, you know, the Hippies."

"Yeah? Hassling how?"

"You know, name callin' and threats, the usual shit. But this; this is the first I've heard of something like this happening."

"You got any idea where they hang out?"

"No, and don't want to know. Maybe some of the regulars you know around here might have an idea," she said, casting her gaze around the area.

"One time this place meant something, you know. It's almost all gone. Now it's drugs, sex, money. Even the kids comin' in with their anti-establishment bullshit are mostly lame. Some come just to piss off their solid middle-class families. Some come lookin' for fun, a place to crash and a free mea,l or to just get laid. A lotta runaways too, I think. Hear the Gren is going the same way." She was referring to Greenwich Village in New York.

She was alluding to the fifties when she and many of the older generation who still lived here were part of the avant-garde...the

Beats. Alas, as Dylan says, the times they are a-changin'.

I pulled out one of my cards and passed it to her.

"Take this. If you hear anything or remember something, call me."

"So, you going after whoever did this?"

I nodded and stood up.

"Why? He's just another old fag."

"Maybe, but he's also a friend."

Rachel looked up at me and after a moment, smiled.

"You're a good man, Murph," she said, slipping my card into the small leather purse slung over her shoulder. She stood as well, leaned in, and gave me a peck on the cheek. "Later, sweet cheeks."

She was right about one thing, I thought, as I headed out of the park. I needed to talk with some of the people I still knew around here. That meant hitting the clubs.

You want to get a solid handle on a neighbourhood and it's going-ons, talk to those who live and work there, especially the waiters, waitresses, and bartenders. They are the best sources of information next to the street hustlers and working girls.

Phil's is one of several neighbourhood bars surrounding the park. Small, seating only around fifteen or twenty at most. It was surprising that Phil still managed to stay open considering the competition around him and continued refusal to change up to attract the new trade. He once told me that he could keep the doors open because he owned the building. It seemed to work out since he always had enough of the locals come in.

"Jesus, Murph. Been a while," Phil said, putting out his big hand as I stepped up to the bar. I needed to start calling in on some of my old haunts again. Too many 'been a whiles'.

"Yeah. Too long, I suppose," I said, feeling the strength of his grip. Phil is a big powerfully built man from long years working the docks and as a teamster. I once heard that he made a bundle from illegal bare-knuckle boxing.

I took a quick look around the room. There were about eight other people sitting about the room, alone or in pairs; none of whom I recognized.

"Beer?"

"Yeah, sure, thanks," I said as he grabbed a glass and pulled the tap.

"So, what brings ya back here?"

"The usual. A case I'm working. I need to get caught up on the latest happenings around the Park," I said as he placed the glass of cold draught in front of me.

"Like what?"

"Whaddya been hearing about a bunch of rednecks up from the south?"

"Yeah. I been hearin' stuff 'bout them. Showed up a coupla months ago, I think. They come in here once or twice a while ago.

Started mouthin' off and messin' with my regulars."

"Messing how?"

"You know, gettin' in their business wantin' ta know if any fags or niggers come in here, stuff like that. I don't cotton to any of that shit, so I got rid of them pretty quick."

"How many of them were there?" I asked.

"'Bout six as I recall."

"Took a chance bracing them," I said, smiling. Phil could handle himself.

"Naw. Punks mostly. All mouth. Only tough as a bunch."

"Anything else you can tell me about them?"

"Most looked like they was in their thirties I'd guess. Heavy accents. Sounded like mountain boys, or backwoods types, if ya get my drift. Lotta swagger and lip. Hear they cruise the area hasslin' the kids, ya know, them ones the paper calls 'hippies'. Hear they been tryin' to recruit people," he said, his voice heavy with disgust. "Way I hear it, the only requirement to join up is ya gotta be ignorant and filled with hate."

"Yeah, sounds about right," one of the men at bar said.

I looked over at the man. He was in his fifties and dressed in work clothes.

"That there is Fred. Works for the Transit Authority. Had a run-in with them a week back," Phil said.

"That's right. They come on the streetcar one night and start in on some kids. Ended with some pushing and shoving until one of them pulled a shiv. Lucky for the kids a cop just came into the car. They got off at the next stop pretty damn quick."

"The cop do anything?"

"Nope. He was alone and there was five of them, so he just let them go."

"Probably smart, especially if they had weapons," I said.

"Yeah, I guess so. But it'd be no great loss if those boys was planted in the ground."

"That's a bit hard," I said.

Fred shrugged and picked up his glass and took a drink.

I looked back at Phil.

"Don't suppose you've heard anything about where they're holed up?"

Phil shook his head, "Not that I heard. But if ya got a minute, I kin make a call to a buddy of mine has a place over there."

"Yeah, I got time, thanks."

Phil came back five minutes later.

"Looks like there's a bar they seem to use regular like called, Benny's. It's up in the Markham area somewhere," he said. "I heard of the place. Has a rep for been pretty rough an' attracts those sorta people."

"Thanks. That's good to know."

I picked up my glass and finished the beer then stood up. I fished out a ten and dropped it on the bar along with my card.

"Thanks for the beer and the info. Do me a favour, you hear or think of anything else, call me." I said. "Keep the change."

He scooped up the bill and stuffed in his shirt pocket.

"You bet."

I checked my watch: four-forty. I had just enough time to make it to my meeting with Detective Holman.

Holman wasn't hard to pick out. If there was ever a man who looked like a cop, it was Detective Art Holman.

He looked to be in his fifties with thinning hair that was greying at the sides. Dressed in a grey suit that had seen a few too many years, white shirt and tie loosened at the neck and a dark grey fedora. He was thick in the middle from too many bad meals and beer. The job had a way of aging some guys, especially the career ones. He had a rugged face that sported the shadow of a day's growth of beard, but it was his eyes that caught you. They were bright, alert, and gave you the feeling that he was seeing everything.

He was sitting at a small table in the corner, a glass of beer in front of him. As I passed the bar, I signalled the bartender to send two glasses over to his table.

"Detective Holman?" I said as I stepped up to the table.

"Uh-huh, and it's Art," he said, pushing a chair at me with his foot.

"Murph," I said, sitting down and extending my hand which he accepted and shook warmly.

"Manny sez you lookin' for a little help." I liked this guy. No bullshit. Right to the point.

A waitress arrived with the two glasses of beer and set them down. I gave her a five-dollar bill, waving off the change.

"He sez you an' Goldman are good buddies."

I nodded, "Yeah. We grew up together and went to the Academy together. Turned out to be a perfect fit for him. Me, not so much."

"I checked you out. Had a hand on a coupla sticky cases. Seems you got a reputation for getting things done. Good work on that business with Mitchell and Tate."

"Thanks. I take it you know Abe?"

"Yeah. We worked together a coupla times." He didn't elaborate and I didn't ask.

"So. Whaddya looking for? Manny jus' said you're lookin' into that old fag who was attacked a few nights ago."

"That's right. Gabe Herschon. He's a friend. According to Manny, the attack wasn't a mugging. Looks like he was targeted."

"Because...?"

"Gabe's gay. And he's a Jew," I said.

"Okay. So you think there's some people out there maybe targeting these people. Any idea who?"

"I've been asking around. Looks like some men have been seen hassling people, especially in the gay community. Heard they're maybe from somewhere down south,"

"Where you gettin' this from? Does Manny know?"

"Yeah. I told him. As for the information, I talked to the bartender at the club where Gage works. He said there were a couple of instances where these guys came in and rousted Gabe. I also talked with a couple of other contacts, same thing."

"Hmm. Yeah. We been hearin' rumbles 'bout these guys."

"So, they're on the FBI's radar then?" I asked.

"Not exactly. Too small and not political."

"So...?"

"So, they ain't puttin' any resources on them."

"I hear a 'but' in there," I said.

"Yeah. They might not be interested, but they ain't Toronto PD. We're interested."

"That mean you got something?"

He picked up his glass and took a drink.

"Not much. Talked to some guys I know at a coupla stations. Seems these guys been busted a few times. Nothin' they could keep 'em on. Mostly, fightin', intimidatin' citizens.

The feds say they got a big operation goin' on down in Mississippi. Somethin' to do with this civil rights business, anyway, they know 'bout these guys. Seems their names have popped up on their list only 'cause of their possible connections with the KKK."

"You'd think they'd have a bigger presence if they were planning on setting up shop here. Can't think what they hope to achieve with so few," I said.

"Yeah. My guess is that they're keepin' a low profile so they don't draw too much attention to what they're up to."

"Yeah, fighting and intimidating everyone is pretty low profile," I said, sarcastically.

"No one ever said these guys were bright."

"Apparently," I said. "I hear they're operating from somewhere in the Queen's Park area which, on its face, is strange considering that's where so many gays hang out and live."

"Uh-huh. That's what we hear too. We asked the local station to check it out. Ain't so strange when ya think about it. Provides them with a full field of targets. They know these people won't fight back or go to the police. Not a lot of trust in gettin' a fair shake. "

"Yeah, I suppose you have a point," I said.

"Seems they been stayin' under the fed's radar, but they think that they might be connected back home."

"Hmm. You know anything about a bar called, Benny's?"

"Where'd you get that name?"

"Same place. Contacts."

"Hmm...good contacts. Yeah, we know 'bout this place. Seems to be one of their waterin' holes."

"The owner one of the faithful?"

"Maybe. Got nothin' sez yea or nay."

Suddenly a thought came to me. "You or the feds have a man inside?"

Holman gave me a hard look.

"Can't say."

Can't, or won't, I wondered.

"Sorry. Just want to make sure I don't step on anyone's toes or blow anyone's cover."

"What you hopin' to do?"

"Get some evidence that Manny can use to bust them."

"Hmm. Why not let Manny and his crew handle this?"

"C'mon. You know as well as I do, this case will be shuffled down the stack of files as more shit comes in. And, like I said, Gabe is a friend of mine. Besides, I got people and options the cops don't have," I said, leaving it at that.

Holman looked at me for a moment then nodded.

"Yeah, well, jus' watch your ass. Way I hear it, these guys are real assholes."

"I will, and thanks. By the way, you want to be in the loop if I catch anything of interest?"

"Thanks, but no. Got enough shit to keep me busy, pass anythin' you get to Manny. If he thinks I need to know, he'll pass it up the pipe."

"Okay."

"By the way, you hear anythin' 'bout Abe packin' it in?"

"Yeah."

"So it's true then?"

"Looks that way. I spoke to him yesterday and he confirmed it," I said.

"Damn. He's a good cop. Funny, I didn't think he was that old."

"He isn't."

Holman slowly shook his head then said, "Fuckin' job."

"Amen." I stood up and offered him my hand which he a took.

"He gave more than some. He's earned it."

"Yeah, he has," Holman said, letting go of my hand.

I turned and left. Time to head home.

Chapter Five

It was Thursday already. The week was moving fast.

I stopped at the hospital to see Gabe before heading to the office. I had enough information except for some specific descriptions which I hoped to get from Gabe. Once I had that I would head to Queen's Park. I might get lucky and find these guys while the sun was up and get what I needed to pass on to Manny. Right. My luck was never that good. Worse case scenario, I would have to take up their trail at the tavern they were known to frequent; a prospect I wasn't looking forward to doing.

The night before, after the kids went to bed, Jane filled me in on what she learned about the KKK. I had asked Maggie to call her to get some background information so I'd have a better idea what I might be up against. I already had a pretty good idea what these people were about from news reports and stories I'd heard. Turns out they'd been around since before the Civil War in one form or another. Initially, they targeted Catholics and Northern carpetbaggers trying to exploit and capitalize on the remains of the South after the war during the Reconstruction. It quickly evolved into what we think of today, namely, an ultra-right wing organization targeting blacks, Jews, Papists. Their most recent incarnation appeared to embrace many of the former Nazi ideals, particularly those pertaining to racial purity. According to current reports, they'd been charged with, and suspected of, a number of murders, mostly black activists and sympathizers.

It was a mystery to me that such an organization could still exist and even thrive in the United States in the twentieth century. Well, maybe not such a mystery, considering all the crap that they were embroiled in these days: Vietnam, the young engaged in anti-everything protests, Civil Rights, Communist witch hunts in Washington with McCarthy's committee. I could see how these guys could slip under the radar, especially since they seemed to operate in such small numbers. What the hell were they doing in Canada?

Some days it was hard to see through the crap pile.

The streetcar pulled into my stop. and I got off at the corner of College and University. The hospital was only a short walk away. When I arrived, I stopped off at the newsstand in the lobby and picked up a couple of papers for Gabe. I wasn't sure what he usually read so I picked out a copy of a small independent Village paper, a copy of

Variety and today's issue of the Globe and Mail.

The Nurse's Station gave me his room number and I headed down the hall, the bundle of papers tucked under my arm.

Gabe was sitting propped halfway up in his bed. His head was wrapped in a white bandage, and I could see that his chest was also wrapped through his pajama top. He was in a room with three other patients. He looked old and worn out but had a bit of color in his face.

"Murph, dear boy," he said, his voice sounded weak. That was his usual greeting for me.

"You're looking a lot better," I said, pulling a chair over to the side of the bed and sitting down. I placed the papers on the side table next to his bed.

"Only hurts when I laugh, as they say," he said, smiling.

"Yeah, funny how they always say something stupid, isn't it? I picked up some papers for you," I said, indicating the pile on the table.

"Thanks, I appreciate it. You just missed Maggie. She stopped in on her way to your office. She said you'd be by. Such a lovely girl." He looked at me and gave me a funny look.

"She said that you're looking into what happened. I know you, Matt. I appreciate what you want to do but I would never forgive myself if something happened to you, especially if it meant your daughters losing their daddy."

He only ever called me Matt when he was being serious.

"Look, you let me deal with that, okay? Besides, you know I can take care of myself, and I won't be taking any chances if I don't have to. I'm only going to get as much information on who did this and pass it on to Gus and Manny."

He knew both men and my connection to them.

"What you plan to do hasn't always turned out to be the same as what actually happens, has it?"

"Yeah, you got me there. So, you feel like talking about what happened?"

He looked at me a moment longer then nodded. I sat quietly and waited for him to begin.

"Since I can't convince you to leave it alone, okay," he said. "Before we start, be a dear and pour me a glass of water. The pitcher is there, thanks."

I poured water into a glass and passed it to him.

"I got most of what happened from the cops," I said, "but that was after the fact. What can you tell about before?"

"I don't remember much, actually," he said, taking a drink of water. "It all happened so fast."

"I understand. Just try. For instance, did these guys brace you before they started in on you?"

"No. What I remember is a car suddenly pulling up to the curb and a couple of men getting out. Next thing I remember is being pushed into an alley."

"So you remember that there were two men?"

"Actually, I think it might have been three."

"What next?"

"All I remember is them calling me names and then they started to hit me," he said, wincing.

"Can you recall anything about these guys, like, age, size, how they dressed? Did anyone say a name, for example?"

He shook his head. "Not really. They all looked the same. Mostly in their twenties, I think, maybe a bit older. I do remember they all spoke with that drawl southerners speak. Oh, wait a sec, I just remembered something; I think I heard one say, Billy something."

"Something like, Billy Bob?"

"Yes...yes, that was it. They use those double names a lot down there, don't they?"

"Yeah, it's pretty common," I said. "Don't really get the point but whatever rings their bell... Okay. You're doing great. I don't suppose you remember anything about the car they were in?"

"Sorry," he said. After a moment, he said, "Wait, yes, I think I remember seeing something on the radio aerial. A flag, I think. Yes, a flag, you know one of those old Confederate things."

"That's great, Gabe. Anything else come to mind?"

I saw that he was starting to look tired.

"Okay, buddy. That's enough. You just lay back and rest up. By the way, is there anyone you want me to contact?"

"Maggie already asked me that. She has the information."

I stood up and placed a hand on his shoulder.

"Okay. Get some rest. I'll be by again later," I said.

He nodded slowly and closed his eyes.

"Thank you, Matt," he said, softly.

It was a nice day for a change, and I needed the exercise, so decided to walk back to the office to consider my next move. There was no way to avoid looking at the tavern, and if so, then the best time would be during the day. I would do that this afternoon.

Kensington Market is located in an area bounded by College Street and Dundas Street W., and Spadina Avenue and Bathurst Street. Its denizens are made up of a multicultural mix, especially Jews. It's most known for its open-air market. Lately, it had become a haven for many people opposed to the Vietnam war. Even so, I thought it a strange choice of location for these guys to hole up in, given their particular brand of prejudice.

I got back to the office around noon. Maggie was on the phone when I stepped inside.

"Uh-huh...yes...he just came in, uh-huh, hang on, I'll transfer you," she said.

I looked at her.

"Abe."

"Okay. Can you bring me a coffee, please?" I said, heading for my office.

Once I reached my desk, I picked up the phone as I sat down.

"Hey, buddy, what's up?"

"Just thought I check in with you, see how you're doing with that business about Gabe," he said.

"It's progressing. Why the interest?"

"Nothing really. Just checking up."

"You sound like a mother hen. You okay? It's not like you to worry."

"I know what you're like."

"Yeah? How's that?" I asked just as Maggie came in and set a mug of coffee on the desk then left, closing the door behind her.

"Never mind."

"Okay, spill. You know something I don't?"

There was a long pause on the line then, "Okay. I've been poking around. Talked to one of our guys downtown. He tells me that there are a couple of beats cops they've been keepin' tabs on. Seems they've been involved in a few situations involvin' blacks, hippies, and others."

"Situations?"

"You know what I'm sayin'; roughin' them up, singlin' them out for spot checks. There've been complaints made against them. So far, there's nothing to suggest that they are part of anything these guys you're looking for are into, but you hear the stories about these people."

"Do I hear an 'and' in there?" I asked, taking a sip of the coffee. Strong. Good.

"Maybe. He said there's a possible connection, you know, a blood connection with some of the people living there. It might be nothing. Like I said, my contact said there wasn't anything to say there is a definite connection, but if there is, it could mean that these guys you're after are covered. Just thought maybe it might be useful if you knew the lay of the land before you went pokin' around."

"Okay. Thanks," I said. "Think your guy would be available for a talk if I need anything?"

"Yeah. I already gave him a heads up." He gave me his name and phone number which I wrote down on pad. Lieutenant Ken Burns with I.A. downtown station."

"Thanks. I talked to a Detective named, Art Holman. He's part of a joint task force set up with the CSIS. Manny set it up."

"I know him. Good cop. Get anything useful?"

"Yeah, a little bit. Said CSIS isn't really looking into these guys but do have them on one of their lists, mainly because of a possible KKK connection. Said to pass anything I get on to Manny."

"Hmm, interesting," Abe said. "If they are connected then you better watch your ass around these guys. They definitely don't play nice."

"So I hear. I talked with Elmore."

"Uh-huh. He gonna watch your back?"

"If needed, yeah."

Abe and Elmore had a strange relationship. Abe saw him as a felon and gangster that needed to be arrested. Over time they'd reached a very strange truce with each other, mostly because of their respective friendships with me.

"So? We still on for the weekend?" he asked, changing the subject.

"Uh-huh. Jane and I were thinking maybe we should get together on Saturday night. Maybe go up to Ts. We haven't been there for a while. Hear they're doing Cajun catfish."

I knew that Abe really like seafood and the fact that our wives get on really well with Thelma, Elmore's wife always made for a great night out.

"Sounds good. I'll mention it to Millie when I get home."

"I imagine she already knows if I know my wife," I said, chuckling.

"Yeah, probably. Later." Then he was gone, and I set the phone back in the cradle.

It was beginning to look like I would have to go back over to Kennsington if I wanted to get these guys.

I opened a drawer and dug out a small black notebook. It contained the names and phone numbers of contacts I had throughout the city's boroughs. It was a short list and not all the names were on the 'right' side of the line.

Over the years, I have had a few run-ins with the mob, nothing serious enough to make their hit list, but enough to get their attention. Toronto, like most North American major cities, had its own underworld. Here in Toronto, they had the sense to stay out of the public eye, not like places such as Montreal.

Abe often said that one of these days, keeping these contacts would cost me. So far, it hadn't. I reached for the phone.

"Hello?" said a woman's soft voice.

"Hi. Is Freddie there?"

"No. Who's calling?"

"An old friend. Can you tell him I called and have him call me whenever he gets back?" I asked.

"Okay, just a minute." I heard her looking for a pen and paper. "Go ahead," she said, a moment later.

"Name's Murphy. Matt Murphy. He can get me at my office," I said, giving her my number. "If I'm not here, have him leave a time and number to call, okay?"

"Okay, that it?"

"Yeah, thanks." I heard a click in my ear as she hung up.

Freddie 'Fingers' Giovanni grew up in the same neighbourhood as Abe and I did. Back then, we were part of a small street gang along with a few other kids. It was something all kids did in every neighbourhood, probably from watching too many gangster movies, or maybe as an unspoken survival strategy. Luckily, ours wasn't too heavy into the criminal side like so many of the others around us. That's not to say we were angels, far from it, but whatever mischief we got up to was, by comparison, minor.

Later, when we grew up, we chose separate paths. Abe and I went straight, while Freddie went the other way, finding a home with the mob, rising through the ranks from soldier to running his own little operation with his own crew. I heard he might have made his 'bones' and was now a 'made' man which meant he killed someone. I hoped it wasn't true.

A half hour later, Maggie buzzed a call to me. It was Freddie.

"Yo, ya called?" was all he said when I picked up.

"Freddie. How you doing? Been a while," I said.

"Uh-huh. Whazzup?"

"What're the chances of a meet?"

There was a momentary pause.

"Because?"

"I need to talk to someone I know who's wired into Kensington; I assume you and Tony are still working together?" I said.

Anthony Mancini was his cousin and ran a similar operation to his in the Kensington area.

"Okay. 'Member Louie's?"

"Uh-huh."

"Four o'clock."

I checked my watch: one o'clock. I had time to head to Little Italy. I decided to take my car this and headed home to get it.

Chapter Six

Louie's was a small neighbourhood diner located at College and Crawford in Little Italy used by the area hoods. It was a popular hang out for mob guys and is considered neutral ground to meet and talk, make deals and so on. I'd been there a few times before when I needed to talk with Freddie Giovanni on past cases.; no respecting hood would be seen with a 'fag'.

Like I said before, Freddie and I go way back to when we were kids, but that's another story. A few years back, I was in the neighbourhood for a meeting with one of his crew when someone from a rival gang made a run on him. I stopped him. I don't know what happened to the shooter and, frankly, don't want to know. I have enough on my conscience. Freddie was grateful and let it be known I wasn't to be touched or hassled.

I was playing a long shot coming here today. I didn't know if Freddie could, or would, shed any light on the whereabouts of the men I was after. The mob usually didn't have any dealings with the gays but in this instance he might. After all, these guys were causing trouble that was sure to bring them to the attention of the authorities and that was something Freddie did not want. I knew he had various business interests in the Kensington Market area with his cousin who ran operations there.

I pulled to the curb and parked. The diner was a half a block away on the opposite side of the street. I spotted the usual collection of thugs milling about the entrance, two sitting beside the entrance; three leaning against a parked Caddie. They were all dressed alike: suits, sports jackets, and fedoras. I assumed he was packing his gun somewhere out of sight. A necessary fashion accessory in the mob world.

I recognized one of the two men sitting beside the entrance. I nodded at him as I walked to the door.

"Well, lookie here, if it ain't the peeper," the man said. "Whatcha doing, slummin'?"

"Hi Mike. Long time," I said.

His name was Mike Clancy, an Irish thug. I knew him from back in the old neighbourhood. This was the new mob: an equal opportunity employer.

"No shit."

"You're looking good. How's Jeannie?"

He started to preen himself a little at the compliment. More out of habit I supposed.

"She's good, man. You? I hear you got yourself hitched," he said.

"Yeah, a couple of years now."

"Any childer yet?"

"Uh-huh, two. Girls."

"Good. Me. Five. Three boys, two girls. Nutin' like family."

"Amen to that," I said.

I'll never understand the gangster mentality. Their lives were spent in a world of crime and violence: coercing people to give over their hard earned money, profiting from the exploitation of women, breaking bones and even murder, yet, they took pride in their families, their homes, their children like the rest of us.

"Whatcha doin' down here?"

"Meeting. Freddie."

"'Fingers', huh? Didn't know you two kept in touch?"

I didn't take the bait and mention why I was meeting with Frankie.

"Not too much."

"Hey, none a my business. Jus' askin'," he said, raising a hand.

Freddie Giovanni was an underworld figure higher up on the food chain than Mike, but not too high, more like middle management, so he knew better than to press me. The organization was no different than any company or corporation when it came to an established pecking order with the notable exception that overstepping one's place could result in a late night trip to a midnight swim in the lake.

"Guess I'll head inside," I said, stepping to the door. "Good to see you again. Say hi to Jeannie for me."

Clancy nodded and turned back to the other man sitting at the table.

Once inside, I headed for the only booth and slipped onto the cushioned seat. I knew from past visits this was Freddie's 'office'. Looking around, I saw about a half dozen people sitting around the small room. No one I recognized. A moment later a cute young woman shimmied over carrying a tray.

"What'll ya have?"

"Coffee. Black," I said, taking off my hat and setting it on the table.

"That it?"

"Yep."

She turned and walked away. She looked good and knew it, which was okay with me.

Freddie Giovanni stepped into the diner about same time as my coffee arrived. He spotted me right away and came over. As he passed the waitress, he said to bring him the same then slid into the booth.

"Freddie," I said, extending my hand.

"Murph," he said, nodding and taking my hand while he cased out the room. "So? Why ya wanna talk?"

"I'm looking for some people suppose to be dug in up in the Market," I said.

"Uh-huh. Who?"

"Three or four southerners. Came up a few months back, I think."

"What's yer interest?"

"They damn near beat a friend of mine to death a few nights back."

"Any particular reason?"

"He's a Jew and gay," I said, taking a pull of my drink.

His coffee arrived. We both watched her walk away.

"Yeah, I heard somethin' 'bout that," he said.

"It was pretty bad. Cracked skull. A few busted ribs."

"An' you're goin' after them?"

I nodded. "Like I said, he's a friend."

"I remember that about you. I had a few scraps where you had my back. I ain't forgot."

"Ancient history. So, you hear anything about these guys?"

"Yeah, maybe. Heard there were some hicks runnin' 'round shootin' their mouths off 'bout how the kikes an' niggers taking over everythin' an' da fags is corruptin' the States and Canada. Shit like that. A bunch a ass holes. Ain't fuckin' with us, so we ignore them."

"I figured as much. But you do know where they are though, right?"

He nodded.

"You willing to share?"

"Yeah. They got a flop on a side street between Oxford an' Nassau jus' down from Spadina. Way I hear it, the area's popular with these yanks comin' up here."

"You know anything about the Klan setting up shop in the area?"

"Been hearin' a coupla rumors."

"And the bosses are cool with that?"

He gave a quick look. Oops, I thought, wrong question.

I put a hand up. "Sorry."

His expression relaxed. "That's okay. Let's jus' say they got an eye on them."

It didn't take a genius to get the message. The mob had no love for these kind of ultra-conservative radical groups, but were willing to do business with them, like selling them guns. Business is business.

"So there won't be any blow back if I take these guys down?"

"Naw. Do what you gotta do. We're cool. I'll let Gin know, an' I gotta let the boss know."

"I understand. Thanks, that's all I wanted to know. By the way, how's the family?"

"Everythin's good. 'Member, Gina? She's on da honor roll at school. She's gonna go far dat one," he said, a definite hint of pride in his voice.

"That's great, man. She was always a smart one."

"That's da God's truth. Don't know where she got it from, not me."

"Hey, don't sell yourself short, Freddie. You gotta have some smarts to make it as far as you have in the life."

"Yeah, 'spose so. But Gina, she's got a different kinda smarts, ya know what I mean?"

I nodded, "Yeah, I guess I do."

"Heard you got yourself yer own family now?"

"Yep. Two girls."

"To family," he said, picking up his glass and raising it up.

"Family," I said, doing the same.

We finished our drinks, and I got up to leave. I shook his hand and thanked him for coming down and passing the information along. I watched as he headed out the door and then went to the bar to settle up.

My next stop was Henry Silvano at the local cop shop.

Silvano and I first met a couple of years back when I was on the hunt for two dirty cops who almost killed Abe. He was a good cop who helped me out and I was hoping he was still willing to help me again.

I parked in the parking lot of the precinct and went inside. It was business as usual: people standing around talking to lawyers and cops, some in cuffs waiting to be booked, some just wanting to make a complaint. I made my way to the duty sergeant at the desk.

When I caught his eye, I asked, "Is Detective Silvano in?"

"Who're you?" he answered, waving off an angry looking man next to me.

"Murphy. I need to talk to him," I said.

"Hey, I was here first," yelled the angry man.

"Keep yer pants on, buddy," the sergeant said, holding up one hand and picking up the desk phone with the other.

After a moment he hung up and turning back to me said, "Yeah, okay. He's...,"

"Yeah, I know the way, thanks."

I headed for the stairs and went to the second floor. The detectives occupied most of the floor along with a couple of administration offices and public facilities. The cells were down in the basement; processing was on the main floor behind the sergeant's desk.

I spotted Detective Silvano, cigarette dangling from his lips, sitting at his desk pounding away on an old Underwood typewriter, stacks of files cluttered his desk. His jacket was on the back of his chair, his hat sat on one the stacks. He was old school, so he wore a shoulder rig for his gun, a Smith and Weston Police Special .38.

"Got a minute?" I asked as I pulled a chair over and sat down.

He stopped typing and looked at me, offering me his hand which I accepted.

"Anything'd be better than this crap. How the hell are ya? Long time."

"Yeah, been a while," I said.

"So? What brings you back? Huntin' someone again?" he said, swivelling his chair and leaning back.

"Funny you should ask," I said.

"Anybody I should know?"

"Maybe. Actually, I'm sorta hoping you might. Whaddya got on some newcomers up from somewhere down south, maybe Mississippi or Kentucky?"

"Oh, them. Yeah, I know 'bout these guys. Real sweethearts," he said, sarcastically.

"Yeah, that sounds like them. What can you share?"

"First, what's your interest?"

"You heard about a man who was beaten over in the Village a couple of nights back?"

"Yeah. Word is it was an old fag or somethin'. Report said whoever did it really tore him up. The other stations have asked to watch for similar incidents. Looks like they're treatin' this as a hate crime. I'm guessin' you think it's these guys, right?"

"Uh-huh. According to everyone I've talked to the general view is that these guys have been running around hassling and targeting gays, blacks, and anyone they figure aren't true blue all white citizens."

"Mmm, yeah, I can see that," Silvano said. "However, they haven't pulled any of that shit over here, as far as we know."

"Figures."

He gave me a quizzical look.

"The mob. Don't imagine they'd put up that kind of crap in the territory," I said.

"And you come to this conclusion...?"

I just smiled.

"Freddie 'Fingers'?"

I continued to smile.

"Thought so. Anyway, whaddya need from me?"

"Actually, you sort of told me most of what wanted to know. But there is one thing, what to do have on a bar called Benny's up in Kensington?"

"Yeah, we know the place. Owned and run by a real sweetheart of a guy. Loves everything white and no tolerance for anything else. Our guys been lookin' at him. Seems he's got some very suspect affiliations."

"Like?"

"Pro Nazis. White supremacists. Fanatic groups like that," he said. "We suspect he's got a wire into the force. Seems there's a possibility some of the uniforms over there have similar views."

"Jesus. Well, that isn't my problem, thankfully. So, that means this owner likely to be a Klansman, or at the very least, sympathetic."

"Uh-huh. I'm guessin' your guys have been seen hangin' out there?"

"Looks that way," I said.

"And you're goin' in there to get them?"

"Not if don't have to," I said.

"Good. 'Cause you might get a very nasty surprise if you do. So, what exactly are ya plannin'?"

"Get enough proof and pass it over to Manny Roderiquez at the 6th. It's his case."

"What you plan to do and what actually happens don't always jibe as I recall," he said.

I just shrugged.

"Yeah, well, I'll back your play as much as I can if you need me to. I take it you got someone watchin' your back?"

I nodded.

"Hmm, yeah, I remember him. he should be enough."

"Usually is," I said.

I wondered what Elmore would think if he knew just how many cops knew about him and his reputation. I didn't think I'd ask him.

I stole a quick glance at the clock on the wall. It was getting late, and I still had to drive back home during rush hour. I stood and thanked Henry for his help.

"Mind if I use the phone?"

"Yeah, sure, use Bill's desk over there. And, hey, keep me in the loop, okay? I'd really like to get these guys off my beat."

"Count on it," I said, stepping over to the empty desk and picking up the phone.

"Hey, baby, it's me. Got anything I need to know?" I said when Maggie answered.

"Oh, hi. No. Nothing new. Where are you?"

"Little Italy police station. But I'm about to head back so you can close up. I'll see you in the morning."

"Okay. Bye," she said then was gone.

Back in the car, I headed for home.

Later that night after the kids were put down, Jane and I sat on the couch watching a bit of TV before turning in; just your average picture of domestic bliss, living the dream. Earlier, I gave her a quick rundown on what I learned over the last couple of days.

"So you think you've found these men?" she asked when she came and sat down next to me.

"Uh-huh. At least I now have an idea where to look for them," I said, putting my arm over he shoulders and drawing her in close. I can never get enough of her closeness, her scent.

"So does this mean you'll be giving this to the police?"

"Unfortunately, no. I haven't got any actual proof yet. I know these are the guys, but I just can't nail Gabe's beating on them. Yet."

"Hmm. Now what?"

"I'm going to find the proof, something tying these guys to that night. Something the cops can act on and take to the Crown Attorney."

"That sounds like it could be dangerous. Will it be?"

"Hope not. But you know me, I know how to deal with that if it comes up. Besides, El has offered to back me up."

"Uh-huh." she said softly, a hint of concern in her voice.

"It's what I do."

"I know, sweetheart. It's just that I worry a little. A wife is allowed to worry a little, isn't she?"

"Uh-huh. A little," I said, kissing her hair. "By the way, you make arrangements with Mrs. Gunther for Saturday night?"

"Uh-huh,"

The ten o'clock news had just come on the TV. We sat listening for several minutes when the reporter said that there had been a reported beating of two young actors in the Queen's Park area late last night...

'Late last night, two unidentified men
were brutally attacked near
a known gay bar in the Queen's Park
area. The police have said
that the young men are known
residents who were working
as actors and models. They are also
known homosexuals.
The police would not confirm if there
was a connection between
this latest assault and the beating of
another man three nights ago.
When asked if this is possibly a targeted
attack against the gay
community, the police refused to
comment. More to follow.'

"Oh my," Jane said when the reporter finished. "Why would people be so mean, so evil?"

I could not answer so I just held her closer.

"Enough of that," I said, softly. "Let's hit the sack so I can take your mind off the bad news, okay?"

"Mmm, sounds like a good idea," she said, shifting so she could stand up. She started walking slowly toward our bedroom. There isn't a sexier sight in the world than watching my wife walk toward the bedroom with sex on her mind.

I got up and turned off the TV and followed behind her slowly undoing my belt.

* * *

A southern Rebel flag was hung on the wall behind a table where three men sat drinking beer in the dimly lit bar. They were all in their early thirties, about the same build and white. They wore loose fitting shirts with the sleeves rolled up over their upper arms, denims, and work boots. One, whose name was, Bobby Lee, was talking to the others, who leaned in, listening intently. Then a moment later they were laughing.

"Did y'all see how that fuckin' fruit cried like a fuckin' baby," Bobby Lee said, laughing, his voice thick with a southern drawl.

"Ha ha ha, no shit," said one of the men. His name was, Jake.

The third man just grunted.

"Oh, yeah, forgot. How're yer balls? Still hurtin'?" Jake said, smirking.

"Fuck you, Jake. Faggot got lucky is all," he said.

"Hey, lighten up, KC, I was jus' joshin' with y'all."

Just then, the bartender came over carrying four bottles of beers.

"Hey, y'all better take it easy for a while," he said, setting the bottles on the table.

"What the fuck you mean?" Jake said.

"I heard the cops are taking an interest. I got a contact on the force. One of us," he said, pulling over a chair and sitting down. "He sez that someone's been askin' 'round 'bout three southern guys."

"That right?" Jake said. "Who is this guy, he tell ya that?"

The bartender shook his head. "No, but he sez this guy ain't no cop."

"Ain't no cop? Then who is he?"

The bartender could only shrug.

"See what y'all kin dig up on this guy and let us know," KC said.

"No sweat. So, how's the recruitin' goin'? Gettin' anyone?"

"Yep. A few. It's tough, what with all these niggers and Jews livin' here. Most the good white folk 'fraid to take a stand and act, but we're gettin' through to them."

"Yeah, we're lettin' 'em know we're standin' up for them," Bobby Lee said.

"Damn straight," Jake piped in.

"Well, y'all remember, someone's got your number an' might come a'lookin'," the bartender said.

"Yeah? Well, iff'n he gets close enough he won't like what he'll find," Jake said as he slipped an evil looking hunting knife from his boot.

Chapter Seven

Saturday night.

T's was really jumping. A trio in from the West Coast was laying out some really great tunes that had the room in a dancing mood. Even Abe and I were up on the floor more than usual, much to the amusement of our wives, who were looking very happy.

Rufus 'Jumbo' Jones, the club's head cook, had promised a dinner of fresh Louisiana catfish and didn't disappoint. It was delicious. Thelma even came over and sat with us during dessert, which the girls liked. The three women got on like a house on fire. The talk was mostly about us, kids, and all that other stuff women talk about. Abe and I were a couple of happy campers sitting there nursing our drinks.

"Okay. Time to spill," I said to him as the girls started to laugh at some private joke.

"You talking about me packing it in?" he said.

"Yeah. That."

"Well, it's true. I already talked to Mike and personnel."

Mike Clark was a Captain on the force and a long time friend of Abe and, to a slightly lesser extent, me. Mike was the one who got Abe his post at Internal Affairs.

"When?"

"I gave them three months, that's when I'll have my twenty years."

"Well, if that's what you want then I'm really happy for you. I take it Millie is happy with this too?"

He nodded, taking a drink from his glass.

"Any idea what you'll do once you're out?"

"Yeah. I'm taking Millie on a one-month tour of Europe. The honeymoon we never really had."

"Sounds good. Then what?"

He shrugged. "I'll think of something."

"You know you could always partner up with me," I said.

He gave me a funny look.

"No, seriously. The work isn't that bad, and the way things are going these days, there's more work coming in than I can handle. If I had a partner, I could take on more cases."

"Thanks, Murph. I appreciate it. Okay if I sleep on it a while?"

"Sure."

"Thanks. By the way, talking about cases, how's that business going with those guys who attacked Gabe?"

"It's going. I'm pretty sure I tagged who they are and even where to find them, but I still don't have concrete evidence to give Gus and Manny to nail their asses."

"Heard they might be the ones attacked a couple more men."

"Yeah. Two homosexuals. Separate attacks. Planning on dropping in on them on Monday," I said.

Just then, Thelma slipped out of the booth and headed for the kitchen.

"What are you two up to huddled over there?" Millie said, a big, beautiful smile on her face.

"Nothing," I said, raising my hands.

"Yeah, sure," she said.

"Well, if must know," Abe said, suggestively, "we were wondering if…"

I spotted a slight tinge of red come into her cheeks as she took his meaning.

"Well, mister, I can think of only one way to find out," she said, a twinkle in her eye.

"I guess that's our cue," I said, looking at Jane who also had a very familiar look in her eye.

* * *

Monday morning I went down to my office. Maggie was already in – as usual – sitting at her desk, shuffling papers; mostly reports and bills.

"Morning, baby," I said as I stopped in front of her desk. "Anything I need to look at before I head out?"

"No. I got everything covered. How was the trip to see 'Fingers'?" she asked, looking up. She knew most everyone in my sphere of contacts.

"Informative," I said.

"That mean you're close to finding these guys?'"

"Maybe."

I turned and headed for my office. There was something I needed to get. A few minutes later, Maggie came in carrying a mug of fresh hot coffee and set it on the desk.

"Oh," was all she said when she saw me pull my pistol from the small safe.

I almost never carry my weapon anymore, even though I am licensed. It's a Smith and Weston Police Special .38; a throwback to my cop days. It was a good gun; easy to carry, and did the job in close quarters.

"Ben called yesterday," she said, ignoring the gun. "Needs a claim looked into. Nothing serious, so, if it's okay with you, I'll handle it. It just a simple follow up with the claimant's doctor and landlord. Probably take a day or two at most."

"Sure, go ahead. I trust you. Thanks," I said, putting the holstered gun on the desk and picking up the mug.

"Will you be back later?"

"Don't know. I'm playing it by ear for now. I'll call in," I said.

"Right," she said then turned and went back to her desk.

I reached for the phone and dialed Gus' number.

"Detective Ferguson," Gus said when he came online.

"Hi, it's me," I said."

"What's up?"

I gave him a quick rundown on what I picked up, including my meeting with Freddie Giovanni, without mentioning his name.

"Been busy," Gus said when I finished.

"You know me," I said.

"No comment. So, why you really callin'?"

"Heard about the two guys who were attacked over near the Park. Sounds like it might've been these guys, so I thought I'd get whatever you can share."

"Yeah, okay. Looks like the same MO. Victims are a coupla homosexuals. Apparently, it was two separate attacks. Both were beat pretty bad, not as bad as Gabe, but bad. According to witnesses that saw one of the attacks, and who were willing to talk, a late model car pulled up and four men got out. They went straight to each target and started in on beating them. Witnesses said, the attack lasted only a few minutes then the attackers got back in their car and split. Anyway, they were taken to hospital and released the same day. Manny's handlin' it because of the connection to Gabe."

"Anything to help identify the car? Like a southern civil war flag on the aerial?" I asked.

"Yeah, as a matter of fact. How'd you know?"

"Gabe. He remembered seeing it on the car his attackers used. Can you give me their names and addresses?"

"Shouldn't, but, yeah, since it's you. Jus' a sec," he said. A moment later he was back. He gave me their names, addresses and phone numbers which I wrote down in my notebook: Kevin James and Leslie Abbott. They both lived near the Park: one on each side. James lived on St. Basil Lane on the east of the Park, and Abbott lived on Harbord St.

"I suppose this means you're gonna talk to them?"

"Yeah, thought I might. Never know, they might be able to give me something. If they do and it pans out, you guys will be the first to know."

"Yeah, well, watch your back," he said.

"Always. Thanks," I said, then hung up.

I thought I'd try and reach these men by phone first and set up a meeting if possible. I had no luck reaching Kevin James, but did with Abbott.

"Hello?" said a weak sounding soft voice in my ear.

"Morning, Are you Leslie Abbott?" I asked.

"Yes. Who's calling?"

"My name is Matt Murphy. I'm a private investigator. I heard about what happened to you and was hoping to talk to you about it," I said.

"Why do you want to talk to me? What's it matter to you?"

"I'm looking for the men that did this to you because they did the same to a very good friend of mine the other night," I said.

"You mean, Gabe?"

"That's right. So, you'll see me?"

"Uh...," he said.

"Look, if it'll help, call the detective you spoke to, he'll vouch for me."

"Uh, no, I...I guess it'll be okay," he said, "since you're a friend of Gabe."

"Great. When would be a good time for you? How about today?"

"Sure, okay, I'm not going anywhere. You know where I live?'

"Yeah," I said. "I'll be there shortly."

"Uh-huh, but I'm not there. I'm staying with a friend." He gave me the address and his friend's name, Julius Conrad. We agreed to meet at two o'clock. I caught a break. His friend had an apartment on St. George Street. He gave me the address.

I hung up and stood, reaching for my holster. I slipped the rig on, adjusting to its fit and weight.

I took the car today because I planned to take a run over to Kensington Market later that afternoon to check out the tavern I was told about. But first, I stopped at the hospital to look in on Gabe.

I found him sitting in a chair by the window staring out at the street below. His head was still wrapped in a thick cloth bandage, as well as his chest. The various bruises looked like they were painful, but he didn't seem to be bothered by them, probably because of the pain killers they had him on.

"Hey, buddy," I said, stepping into the room and dropping the papers I'd picked up in the lobby on his bed. "Looks like you're feeling better."

"Murph, dear boy" he said, his voice sounding stronger, "good morning."

"Thought I'd stop by see how you're doing. Good to see you out of the bed and sitting up, though I'd've thought it's got to hurt."

"Uh-huh, a little," he said. "Amazing little pills they give you these days. The doctor wants me to start moving a bit and sitting up instead of lying in bed all day."

"Well, guess he knows best," I said.

"How are you doing looking for those men?"

"Getting there," I answered.

"You know you don't have to, Matt. I mean, I appreciate it and everything but..."

I raised a hand and said, "I'm not doing it because I have to."

He smiled. "I know."

"So, you been getting any visitors?"

"Oh, yes. There have been quite a few who have dropped by, you know, from the neighbourhood. Some have brought me flowers and chocolates. Sweethearts, all."

"I wanted to ask, have you got anyone to help you once they cut you loose from here?"

"Uh-huh, thanks for asking. I have made arrangements to stay with a couple of sweet boys for a few days then I'll head back to my place. They have a place on just down the street from my place. They promised to look in on me and take care of my needs once I'm home."

"That's good. You got some good people behind you."

"Thank God for that," he said.

"Well, I guess I'll leave you to rest up. I'll be back again soon. By the way, they say how much longer you'll be here?"

"The doctor said that if everything keeps going like it is, I could be out in about a week."

"Great. Remember, if there's anything, anything at all you need, call Maggie, okay?"

"I will, thank you. And, Matt. Be careful."

"I will."

I left about fifteen minutes later and headed for my interview with Leslie Abbott.

I checked my watch, twelve o'clock. I had time for a quick lunch. I found a small diner near the hospital, parked the car, and went in. I went to the counter and ordered a club sandwich and coffee. I took the time to work out a plan of action. I flexed my shoulders to adjust to the strap and weight of the gun which still a little uncomfortable.

I arrived at the apartment on St. George Street at one-fifty. It was in a two-story wood house built in the Victorian style like so any in the area. I went up the steps to the door and rang the bell to Conrad's apartment. It was on the second floor.

"Hello? Who is it?" a voice crackled through the intercom.

"Murphy," I said.

"Second floor."

A moment later I heard the lock click and opened the door.

At the top of the flight of stairs I saw a man in his forties dressed in slacks and a casual shirt standing in a doorway.

"Mr. Abbott?" I said, stepping toward him.

"No. I'm his friend, Julius Conrad. You're Mr. Murphy? The private investigator?"

"Uh-huh," I said, pulling out my wallet and flipping it open for him to see my licence. He took it and carefully look at it for a moment then handed it back, opening the door to his home. I stepped inside.

Leslie Abbott was sitting on the sofa looking the worse for wear; his face showing two very angry looking bruises and one eye covered by a gauze pad, the other, red from a burst blood vessel.

He looked to be in his early twenties. Despite the bruises, it was easy to see that he was a very good-looking young man. He was slightly built, like a lot of young male models these days.

"Please, sit down. Can I get you anything? Tea? Coffee?" Conrad asked.

"No, thanks. I'm good," I said, sitting on the sofa chair.

"Thanks for talking to me," I said to Abbott."

"That's okay," he said. "I know Gabe. He's a good person and, well, as they say, any friend of his is...well...you know."

I nodded. "You feel up to talking about what happened to you?"

"Yes."

"Good. Now, just tell me in your own words what happened."

Conrad had come over and sat close to him on the sofa, placing a hand on his thigh.

"It all happened so fast. I was walking home from a small party at a friend's place. There weren't too many people out, so the street was fairly empty."

"What time was this?" I interrupted him.

"About two, I think."

"Okay. Go on."

"I was just walking past an area that was kind of dark. The streetlight was out. Suddenly, out of nowhere, a man grabbed me from behind and started to drag me into an alley. Once we were inside the alley, other men appeared and they started calling me names and pushing me."

He stopped and lowered his head. He started to tremble, and I thought he was crying.

"There, there. It's okay. You're safe now," Conrad said, putting an arm around his shoulders.

"Must he go on?" he said to me.

"No. No, it's okay. I want to talk about," Abbott said, his voice shaky but I could hear the anger in it.

"If you're sure," I said.

Abbott nodded and the continued. "A few minutes later, one of the men started to make awful suggestions about doing things to me. They all laughed. I managed to break free for a moment and kicked one of them in the groin as he was unbuckling his belt. That's when another one started to punch me. I must have started to scream because a few minutes later they let me go and took off."

"Do you happen to remember anything about these men? Anything at all?"

"They smelled. You know, body odour. I think they'd been drinking as well. And they all spoke with that funny way southern people have, you know, twangy."

"Hmm. So, you're saying that these guys were hiding in that alley?"

"Yes, well, uh, most of them. There was one man who was standing outside leaning on a car, now that you ask. I guess he was the one looking for someone like me to come by.”

“The car. Do you remember anything about it?”

“'Fraid not. I'm not really a car person, however, I think I remember seeing a small flag or something on it's aerial.”

It was the same car. I was sure of it.

“Okay. That about covers everything I need to know. Thanks again for talking to me and I'm really sorry about what happened to you,” I said, standing up.

“I hope it helps. Are you going to find these people?” he asked, looking up at me.

“I plan to, yeah,” I said.

“Good,” he said. “I hope you hurt them...I mean, really hurt them.”

His friend stood and walked me to the door.

“I hope you find these bastards and...,” he said, choking back his anger.

“Yeah,” was all I could say.

Once back on the street, I headed for my car. It was time to take a run over to Kensington and pay a visit to Benny's. These guys were really starting to piss me off. But first, I had to check in with Maggie. I found a payphone nearby.

“Good. You called,” Maggie said, when she answered the phone.

“What's up?”

“Elmore called. Said he needed to tell you something. He's at the restaurant.”

“Okay, thanks,” I said, “that it?”

"Yes."

"Okay. Finish up what ever you're doing then lock up for the day. See you tomorrow."

I hung up then dropped another dime and dialed.

"T's," a sexy sounding woman's voice said into my ear.

"It's Murphy. Can you put me through to the man?"

"Hang on," she said.

A moment later. "Yo."

"You called?" I said.

"Yeah. Jus' wanna give y'all a heads up. Looks like them crackers fucked up and offed a brother. An ole man."

"Yeah? Are they...?" I started to ask, thinking the worst.

"Naw. They fucked off 'fore we could get our hands on them."

"Okay, so why you telling me?"

"Jus' wanna let y'all know that the brothers are on the hunt for them jus' in case you cross paths."

"Okay, thanks. They know I'm also looking?"

"Uh-huh. I let them in on your action. Summa the brothers know y'all, so you cool."

"I appreciate that," I said.

"Them muthas better hope you find them first," he said.

"I understand. I won't get in their way," I said.

"Figured as much. Later."

Okay. Now this situation was getting deadly serious. If Elmore's people found these guys before I did, there would be three more bodies found in an alley or the Don River. I made another call.

"Sergeant Ferguson," Gus said when he picked up.

"Hi, it's me," I said.

"What's up?"

"I thought I'd better give you a head's up to pass on to Manny. I just learned that our guys may have killed an elderly black man and now certain people are looking for them."

"Let me guess, Jackson?"

"Does it matter where I got the information?"

"I guess not. Thanks. I'll pass it along to Manny when he gets in. Never know, might be a quick an' easy solution to the problem, they find these guys first."

"That's one way to look at it, yeah," I said.

"Yeah. Anything else?"

"Nope. That's it. I'm heading back to Kensington soon as I hang up. I get anything worth sharing, I'll call."

"Good luck and watch your back."

"Always," I said then hung up. Time to go.

Chapter Eight

I thought about how I was going to approach the tavern on the drive over to Kensington Market. So far, I had the edge: they didn't know about me, or at least I hoped they didn't because, by all accounts, I could be walking into a world of hurt. The gun under my arm suddenly felt very comforting. It wasn't like I wasn't used to dealing with hard cases or situations. I've had my share, so I wasn't exactly a novice, or unaware about what might be waiting inside.

I arrived on Nassau Street and spotted the tavern about half a block away on the left side of the street. I pulled the car into an empty parking space, opting to park the car and walk the rest of the way. It would give me the chance to scope out the street. No big surprises. The street was moderately busy with people and traffic moving about. Most of the people looked like you'd expect: average folks coming and going, doing their usual daily routines; go to work, go home, shop. I scanned the parked cars looking for one with a flag on it's aerial. None. I crossed over to the other side and approached the entrance of the tavern and went in.

It was what I expected: your standard neighbourhood tavern. There were eight people sitting around the room at various tables with drinks on them. Mostly, they were men who looked like working stiffs having a cold one on the way home or out of work and killing time. Two women sat at one of the tables; shopping bags sitting beside them on the floor. It looked like every bar I'd ever been in, except for the Confederate flag that hung on the wall at the far end of the room above a single table, where a solitary man sat with a glass of beer. Guess I was in the right place.

The bartender walked down to where I sat. He carried a wet cloth and had a cigarette hanging from the corner of his mouth. I guessed him to be in his fifties. He was short and balding with a bulging stomach that hung over the waist of his pants.

"What'll ya have?" he said, the cigarette bouncing as he spoke.

"What's on tap?" I asked.

"Molson's."

"Works for me," I said, taking my hat off and setting it on the bar.

A moment later he came back with my beer.

"You ain't from aroun' here are ya?" he said, setting the glass on the bar.

I picked it up and took a drink.

"Nope."

"Don't get many strangers in here."

"That so."

"Hey, no offence, buddy. Jus' makin' small talk is all," he said, raising a hand.

"Yeah, sorry," I said. "Been one of those days. Just came from a long meeting with a coupla assholes. I was heading back to the office and must've taken a wrong turn somewhere. Saw your place and decided to stop for a cold one before going back."

"Yeah, easy to get turned around. What line ya in?"

"Tools. I'm a sales rep for a tool company. They got a coupla service stations they sell to."

"Ah," he said, with a nod. "Any luck?"

"I'll be able to pay the rent for a coupla more months," I said, smiling. "Say, I couldn't help noticing the flag back there. You don't sound like a southerner."

He turned and looked at the flag and said, "Ain't. A lotta them boys have moved up here. Duckin' Uncle Sam an' a trip to 'Nam. They come in here a lot, so I put it up to make 'im feel at home, ya know? Started 'bout eight months back, I'd say."

"My name's Garry," I said, extending my hand.

"Max, Maxie to my customers," he said, accepting my hand.

"Nice to meet you."

"Thanks, you too. Another one?"

"No, better not. I gotta drive, maybe next time I'm back over here. I usually make a sales call every month or so. Thanks for the beer. See ya," I said, sliding off the stool. I didn't want to push it yet. Better to keep it on the down low for now. I had found out what I needed. This was the place I'd find my guys.

I had worked out a general plan of action. First, I'd stakeout the place and wait for these guys to show up, then wait for them to leave and follow them. If I got lucky, I'd catch them in the act then take them down. Risky, but I couldn't think of anything better short of Elmore's people getting to them first which would mean a midnight swim in the lake or a long ride out of town to a patch of woods. Problem with that idea was obvious.

* * *

The man sitting at a table near the back of the room, watched Maxie and me talking. He didn't like strangers suddenly showing up. Especially now, since learning that there was someone looking for him and the others. Ten minutes passed before the man got up and left. He waited a minute longer then went to the bar.

"Who was that?"

"Huh? Who?" Maxie said as he poured another glass of beer from the tap.

"Him. The guy you was talkin' to, who else?"

Maxie placed the glass on the bar in front of him.

"Nobody. Just a salesman made a wrong turn an' come in for a beer. Why?"

"Jus' don't like strangers comin' round is all, 'specially since y'all said someone's been snoopin' an' all."

"Jesus, Jake, lighten up will ya. This is a fuckin' tavern for Chrissake. People gonna walk in, right? Even people we don't know."

"Yeah, well, what'd he want?"

"A fuckin' beer."

"Don't smartmouth me, hear, boy?" Jake said, anger creeping into his voice.

"Hey, take it easy. He didn't ask any questions 'bout anything. Jus' made casual talk. He's sez he's a salesman. Sell tools. Was up here sellin' tools to suma the service stations an' made a wrong turn on his way back ta where he came from, saw my sign an' stopped for a cold one. Okay?"

"Yeah, okay. I jus' don't like the look of him."

"So, how're you guys doin' now? You know, with the recruitin'?" Maxie asked, hoping to change the subject.

"We're gettin' some people on board. Place is ripe for gettin' new members. Lotta folk unhappy with all these immigrants comin' in an' takin' over everything. Lotta them 'specially worried 'bout all this civil rights horse shit going on with the niggers back home."

"You think there's a lot the Brotherhood can do?"

"Don't know, this ain't down south. White folk up here not the same as them back home."

Maxie nodded but didn't say anything.

"You still in touch with that cop y'all told us about?"

"Yeah, why?"

"See iff'n he can get anymore information on what the cops are doing 'bout our business."

"Okay. I'll make a call. Might be a day or two before he calls back."

"That's okay. Jus' keep us in the know."

Jake took his beer and went back to his table to wait for the others to come back. They had plans for tonight.

About a half hour later, a uniformed cop entered the bar and went to where Maxie sat behind the cash register reading a paper. They spoke for several moments then the cop turned and left.

Jake watched this exchange and once the cop was gone, he stood and went to the bar.

"What was that about?" he asked, sitting on a stool, and taking a pack of cigarettes from his shirt pocket.

"That was my contact with the police," Maxie said.

"Figured that out. What'd he say?"

"A coupla things. Bad news. KC was fished outta the lake this morning. Looks like he was beat pretty bad before someone shot him in da head."

"What! Shot? Who...?"

"Don't know."

"What else?"

"Got a name on da guy nosin' around. Murphy. A gumshoe from over in da Village. Word is he's lookin' for them that roughed up that faggot a coupla nights back. I guess that's you guys."

"Okay, okay, let me think," Jake said.

"What're gonna do 'bout KC?"

"I said, let me think," Jake snapped.

After a moment, he said, "Cain't do anythin' 'bout KC. The cops'll probably figure it out an' git in touch wit his kin. The bigger problem is this Murphy fucker. Chances are the cops don't know 'bout the rest of us, but this guy might, an' if he does, he might put two an' two together an' tell the cops."

"Sounds likely," Maxie said.

"Okay. Me an' Bobby Lee gonna lay low for a bit 'an stay away from here. You git anything, call us at the boardin' house, got it?" Maxie nodded.

"So what ya gonna do 'bout the snooper?"

"Y'all don't fuss 'bout that. We'll deal with him," Jake said. "Meantime, y'all lean on that cop there, an' git as much information on Murphy as he can, 'an git it to us."

"Yeah, sure thing," Maxie said, nodding. "Like I said, might take a day or two."

"Don't care, jus' git it."

Jake sat thinking for several minutes.

"Ya don't think Murphy did KC, do ya?" Maxie asked.

"Huh? Don't know. Why would he?" Jake said, coming back.

"Jus' wonderin'."

"Somethin' else you kin git the cop to find out. Is Murphy a killer?"

"Okay. Uh, ya know it could maybe be the niggers 'cause of that old man ya did?"

"Hmm, yeah, maybe," Jake said.

"Maybe it's time to pack up an' get outta town for a while."

Jake shot him an angry look.

"Fuck that. Ain't gonna be pushed around by any fuckin' niggers or a faggot lover."

"Jus' a suggestion," Maxie said.

Jake stood up and started for the door.

"Y'all jus' keep gittin' me what I need ta know. Bobby Lee comes in tell him I'm back at the digs."

"Okay. See ya," Maxie said, watching him exit through the door. He was sympathetic to their cause, but this could get real expensive and...dangerous.

Later, back at the apartment, Jake and Bobby Lee sat at the kitchen table, each with a bottle of beer. The ashtray sitting in the middle of the table was full of stubbed cigarette butts.

"Whaddya figure happened ta KC?" Bobby Lee asked when Jake finished filling him in.

"Don't know. Whoever did this didn't do it alone. KC was no pussy. Had to be someone knew him."

"Jesus, that means we could be next."

Jake just sat looking at the bottle in his hand for several moments.

"What're we gonna do now?" Bobby Lee asked, breaking the momentary silence.

"We're gonna keep on with the plan, that's what," Jake said, picking up his beer and taking a drink.

"Yeah, okay, but what 'bout all this attention seems ta be on us, 'specially this peeper, fella? Near's we kin tell, the cops don't know 'bout us, else we'd been picked up by now. So, that means it's jus' this Murphy asshole. We take him out, maybe we'll be okay," Bobby Lee said.

"Hmm, maybe," Jake said, thinking.

"We know anythin' more'n his name?"

"Maxie's lookin' inta it. Once he's got somethin' then we'll make us a plan."

"Amen ta that," Bobby Lee said, raising his bottle.

Chapter Nine

It was time to check in with Manny Rodriquez.

Traffic was as expected: heavy. Sitting between two cabs, I remembered why I didn't drive in the city if I could help it. It had started to cloud over, and the air felt close with the possibility of rain. People scuttled along the sidewalks hoping to get to their destinations before the sky opened up.

I finally made it to the station at twenty-past-five. I pulled around to the side of the building where the squad cars and the private cars of the duty cops parked. I knew Gus didn't drive his own car, so I headed into the slot assigned to him. I usually parked there. When I got out and headed for the front, I spotted a couple of older beat cops I recognized. They had a couple of younger uniforms with them.

"Hey Joe, what's shakin'?" I said, as I neared them.

Joe Kelsey was a twenty-year veteran of the force, all of it on the street as a beat cop. He was old school and had a solid reputation as an honest and fair officer both on his beat and among his peers, but he wasn't a push over.

"Hey Murphy," he said, "ya know, same ole shit. Whatcha been up to?

"Lou," I said to the other man I knew. He just nodded and continued on his way with one of the younger cops in tow.

"Don't mind him," Joe said. "We're baby-sittin' some new guys for a coupla days, and he don't like it much."

"Hey, he was a rookie once," I said.

"Yeah? When was that?" he said with a chuckle. "What brings you here? Ain't seen much of ya since Abe moved over to HQ."

I caught the young cop eyeing me. I suppose he was trying to figure out if I was someone important.

"Got some business with Manny," I said. "I assume he's in?"

"Yeah, I think I saw him come in 'bout fifteen minutes ago."

"Thanks. By the way, how're Charlotte and the kids?"

"Everythin' is as it should be, I suppose. Bill, my oldest, is in his second year at Ryerson. Studyin' engineering."

"That's great, Joe."

"Thanks. So, how 'bout you? Hear ya got two kids now."

"Uh-huh. Two girls," I said, smiling.

"Funny how that happens, ain't it. Well, guess we better hit the bricks. Nice to see ya," he said as he turn and headed away.

"Yeah, you too. Say hi to Charlie for me."
Charlie was his nickname for his wife.

"C'mon youngster. Time to introduce ya
to the street."

I headed for the main entrance at the
front of the building. The main reception
area was a zoo, as usual: hooked up felons,
people with complaints, lawyers trying to get
to clients; everyone talking at the same time
creating a pulsating drone.

I caught the desk sergeant's eye and
pointed upstairs. He recognized me and
nodded.

It was the shift change so when I entered
the squad room, men were in the process of
coming and going. I spotted Manny sitting at
Gus's desk. Probably going over files. I
waved at Gus when he looked my way then
pulled a chair over to Manny's desk and sat
down to wait for him to finish up with Gus.

Ten minutes later, he came over and sat
down, followed by Gus, who was pulling on
his overcoat.

"Gentlemen. Glad to see you getting
outta here early for a change," I said, looking
up at Gus.

"Yeah. One of the kids is in a play over at
one the clubs. First time. Delores and I are
going," he said, smiling. Delores was his
wife. One of his kids, a son I think, got the
acting bug.

"Yeah? Well, say hi to Delores for me and
hope the kid does well."

"Me too. Anyway, you got something I need to know 'bout?"

"Not yet. I think Manny and I can deal with it for now" I said.

"Okay. See ya later."

"So? Whaddya got?" Manny said when Gus was gone.

"I just came back from Kensington. I was checking out that local these guys suppose to be using. It's called Benny's. On Nassau a block and a half up from Bathurst. I'm pretty sure this is where these guys are hanging out; spotted a Confederate flag hanging at the back. May be nothing more than a coincidence, but... I had a short chat with the guy works there, name's Maxie, said there were quite a few southerners in the area. Seems they favour his place. Might explain the flag."

"Uh-huh. You didn't happen to spot these guys by any chance?" Manny asked.

"No, and I didn't press. Not yet. Didn't want to tip my hand in case they don't know about me. I plan to go back and stake out the place."

"How're you gonna know who to tail, since you haven't fingered any of them yet?"

"I got a solid lead on their car. Watch for that and, bang, I got them."

"Okay. Jus' watch yer ass."

"Not a problem," I said, pulling my jacket open, exposing the shoulder rig. "Covered."

"Gus tells me that yer buddy passed the word that some of the brothers are gettin' involved since they found that old black man that was found dead. Got anythin' to add?"

I shook my head.

"Jus' so ya know, I passed this along to some of the other stations in the area. They needed to know 'bout this in case it gets fuckin' messy."

"Good idea. It gets to being a shooting match a lotta people could get hurt. Hopefully, I'll luck out and get something you can use to nail these bastards before it gets to that stage."

"Gotta ask, Murph. You keepin' yer buddy in the loop?"

"No. Like you, last thing we want to see are the blacks running around looking for heads to take. Doesn't do anyone any good. Besides, he was just passing some information on."

"Okay."

"You got anything new?"

"Not much. We've been interviewin' people in the area of the attacks for any possible leads. All we got so far is that it's three or four men, late twenties to mid thirties, white. There's also some agreement about the car. I take it this is the same car you mentioned?"

"Probably."

"When ya planning to start?"

"Tomorrow night."

"Going solo?"

"Yeah," I said, nodding, "at least for a couple of days. If I can't shake up something by then I got someone I can call to help out."

"Keep in touch an' watch yer back," he said.

Nice how everyone was always worried about me watching my back. I got up and headed for the parking lot then home.

The next day I headed for the office. I listened to the news on the radio before leaving home waiting to hear anything on another attack. Nothing. I stopped at a newsstand, picking up a couple papers before getting on the subway. Again, nothing. Looks these guys had taken a night off.

"Mornin', boss," Maggie said when I arrived.

"Mornin'," I said.

"How're things going with your search?"

"There going. How'd you make out on that business for Ben?"

"Piece of cake. Looks like the claim is legit and will go through. I'm going to cut an invoice later today for two days."

"Good work, baby. I knew you could do it."

"This keeps up you might have to make me a partner," Maggie said, smiling.

"Well, maybe a raise at least. Listen, speaking of partners, you know Abe's put his papers in, right?"

"No, I didn't know. When?"

"About a week ago. I thought I told you. Anyway, he's finished in a coupla months. He's gonna take Millie to Europe for a honeymoon. I told him he had a place here with us when he got back."

"That's great. I like Abe. He'd be a good addition to the operation," she said, sounding genuinely happy at the idea. She and Abe got on really well.

"No hard feelings then? I know you've been doing this for a while and maybe..."

Maggie raised her hand to cut me off, then said, "Don't be silly. I like my job here just fine. Now, what was that you said about a raise?"

I laughed.

"Let me work it out, okay. But, yeah, I was thinking you've earned one."

"Thanks, Murph. Coffee?"

"Yeah," I said then headed for my office.

About an hour later Maggie buzzed a call through to me. It was Detective Henry Silvano over in Little Italy.

"This is a surprise," I said, picking up the phone.

"Somethin' jus' came in," he said into my ear, ignoring my comment. "Thought you'd like to know."

"Shoot."

"Funny you should say that. Seems a body was fished outta the lake early this mornin'. White guy, mid to late twenties maybe. coroner sez he was beaten pretty bad before he took a single shot to the head.

Looks like whoever did him was pretty damn serious about wantin' to hurt him."

"And this is of interest to me why?" I said.

"Near's as anyone can tell, the victim wasn't a local. No one could ID the guy. They did find a wallet. Only thing in it was some papers, a few bucks, a driver's licence and, oh yeah, a card with the Confederate flag printed on it. Looks like a membership card or somethin'."

"Now that is interesting," I said, sitting up. "Got a name?"

"Yeah. James Robert Clarkson. Mean anythin'?"

"No. But I'm guessing you're thinking that he might be one of the guys I'm looking for, right?"

"Possibly, yeah. You think it might be one of these assholes Manny warned me about?"

"It's possible."

"Yeah, well, thought I'd let you know. By the way, you got anythin' new since we last talked?"

I filled him in quickly on my visit to the Benny's and my hunches. I also told him my plan.

"Okay. Thanks, and watch it. The game's startin' to get deadly."

The news suddenly changed everything. If the body is one of the guys I'm looking for, then the others would be either on the run or gone to ground. It had to be done by the people Elmore warned me about. I was curious how they managed to find one of them so quickly, however, I wasn't going to call him and ask.

My thoughts were interrupted by the buzz of the intercom.

"Yeah?" I said, pressing down the switch.

"Gus is on the line," Maggie said.

"Okay, thanks," I said, picking up the phone.

"What's up?" I said.

"Just went over Manny's reports. I see here that he got a call from Silvano. Seems they found a body this morning in the lake. Seems this body is a guy from Mississippi. Care to comment?"

"Yeah, I heard from him as well. Can't add anything to what you got," I said.

"Look, Murph, you know as well as I do, if this is one the guys you're after then it's a good bet that he was taken out by one of your pal's people. If so, then he's gonna need to get himself a good lawyer."

"What for? I'm pretty sure he isn't behind whatever's happening," I said.

"Gee, that makes me feel a whole hellava lot better," he said, sarcastically.

"Seriously. He isn't behind any of this. When he called me, he said that word on the street was that some of the brothers, probably from one of the more action groups who decided to take this matter in hand and went looking for these guys"

"Yeah, okay, maybe. But tensions are high around here right now. Every day we're gettin' calls to put out brush fires all over the city and headquarters is looking for any way to defuse the situation."

"Gotcha."

"Look. I'm gonna share somethin' with you on the QT, got it?"

"Sure," I said.

"We've suspected for a while that there was a group of southern agitators stirrin' up shit all around the city for about the last eight to ten months. We haven't been able to catch any of them in the act because of how they're operatin'," Gus said, his voice down a level or two.

"Let me guess. Two to four men doing random attacks on various people."

"Close enough. They have been mostly targeting the gays and hippies, but lately, been goin' after blacks."

"I get why you're concerned," I said.

"Right. Now it looks like you might've stumbled onto somethin' that's had us puzzled."

"Yeah? What was that?"

"Where were these people operatin' from? We couldn't nail anything down since all the attacks appeared to be random and spread over too many areas."

"Kensington," I said. "You think these people could be operating out of the there?"

"Maybe, if what you've picked up on is accurate. I think it's maybe time you think about steppin' away and let us handle this."

"No can do, Gus. You know I can't, or won't."

"Why do you always hafta make things so fuckin' personal, huh?"

"It's who I am. You, more than anyone, should know and understand that," I said.

"Yeah," he said, after a brief pause. "I haven't forgot what you did for Abe and why."

There was a momentary silence before he spoke again.

"Well, it's your ass, so watch it."

"Don't I always," I said.

"Right."

"Oh, yeah, almost forgot. I talked with Abe on the weekend. Looks like he's definitely packing it in. Thinks he'll be a civilian in a couple of months. Plans to take Millie to Europe for a month."

"Yeah, I know," Gus said.

"I offered him a partnership with me when he gets back."

"Hmm. That'd be a good fit."

"I think so. It's in his court for now. Said he'd consider it and get back to me when he's back. By the way, how was the kid's debut?"

"Went pretty good. He didn't have a major part, but he pulled it off. Remembered all his lines and everythin'. Pretty proud of him."

"I bet. Talk to you later," I said then hung up.

I made a decision and picked up the phone and dialed.

"T's," a sweet sounding female voice said in my ear.

"Hi, it's me, Murph. Is he in?" I said, dispensing with my usual banter.

"Yeah, jus' a sec."

A moment later Elmore came on the line.

"Whazzup?"

"Thought you'd like to know that they fished a body out of the lake. White guy from the South. Beaten pretty bad before taking a single shot in the head."

"Yeah, so? What's one dead cracker ta me?"

"Cops suspect it might be somebody from your neighbourhood."

"Why'd they figure that, I wonder?"

"Yeah, I kind of gave them a head's up that people were looking for these guys. No names or anything like that, but they know me pretty well and put two and two together."

"Meanin' they know 'bout me?" Elmore said.

"Uh-huh. So you might be getting a visit. Thought I'd better give you a head's up. I did my best to keep you out of it, okay?"

"Y'all had to tell them, right?"

"Look, I'm not gonna apologize for wanting to avoid any sort of blood bath. You more than anyone, knows what'll happen if these guys swarm into the Market and force a confrontation. If that happens a lot more than those guys will get hurt. For what it's worth El, I think I put them off of you. Okay?"

There was a long silence then, "Yeah. We cool. Thanks for the head's up."

The line went dead. I knew he wasn't mad or angry with me. I knew he agreed with me, but sometimes I couldn't help but wonder just how far I could go with him before he did lose his cool. So far, we hadn't reached that point.

Around midday, I decided to head out for a quick bite. Maggie had left for the bank to deposit a couple of cheques that arrived in the morning mail. I left a note on her desk saying where I went in case she came back before me then I locked up.

It was a nice day for a walk. About a block away from my office I spotted the tail.

He was on the opposite side of the street staying close to the buildings as he walked slowly along trying to not look conspicuous. He didn't realize just how much he stood out dressed as he was in an open neck shirt, jeans, and a zip up jacket. Once I realized I had a tail and got a look at him, it was clear I'd lost my edge of anonymity and that made me worry. How long had they known and how much did they know? I couldn't let myself worry about that now. I had to decide what to do about the immediate problem.

Should I lose him? Reverse the tail? Isolate and confront him?

The last option wasn't a good idea since it was midday and there really wasn't any place I could lead him into without drawing attention. I also wasn't too keen on giving him the slip so that left only one option.

Luckily, I knew this neighbourhood like the back of my hand and could easily turn the tables on him, setting him up to lead me back to where he came from.

I continued down Spadina for another block to an alley I knew that opened into a large vacant space behind several buildings. One of the buildings backing on this space had a rear door that usually wasn't locked during the day that I could use to get back to the street. That would put me behind him.

I needed some way to duck into the alley without him seeing me go. The gods must have smiled down on me because just at that moment a delivery van rounded the corner ahead of me. I walked slowly toward the alley timing my steps so that I could duck in as the van passed by, cutting off my tail's view for a few seconds.

Once in the back court area, I made my way to the door I knew was unlocked and went inside. The hallway went straight to double glass door at the front of the building. I stood in the deep shadows looking out at the street trying to find the tail. He wasn't anywhere in sight. I decided to take a chance and step outside for a better look.

Fortunately, the door was recessed by three feet so I could stay partially out of sight.

Looking down the street, I spotted him standing still on the opposite side of the street. He was looking up and down, obviously trying to find me. After several minutes, he gave up and flagged a passing cab which he got in when it pulled to the curb.

'Damn it,' I thought, I hadn't anticipated that. There was no point in trying to catch up to him now. The traffic was too busy, and I didn't think I could get a cab fast enough before losing sight of him, so I continued on to the deli. I had to reconsider my plans now I was aware they were on to me. So much for easy. Now it would be as it always seems to go with me, I thought, as I heard the faint chuckle from on high. I have long held the belief that I have a special relationship with the gods that seem to have taken an interest in my life. Every so often they toss a couple of 'hiccups' into my life and I, for my part, provide their entertainment as I try to survive them.

Must still be fun for them because, after all, I'm still kicking.

Chapter Ten

When I returned to the office, Maggie wasn't at her desk. My first reaction was that they got to her. Since picking up the tail I'd been on edge. But the feeling disappeared when I spotted the message taped to my office door –

Murph, gone to an appointment. Be back by two.

Also, Det. Silvano called. Wants to talk to you ASAP.

There's a fresh pot on the element. M.

I poured a cup of coffee and went into my office and called Silvano.

"Detective Silvano's desk," someone said into my ear.

"It's Matt Murphy returning his call," I said.

"Oh, yeah. He's out on a call. But he left a message for ya, jus' a sec." I heard a soft thud as he set the phone down followed by the sound of papers being moved around.

"Yeah, here it is. It sez ta tell ya that you're blown."

"That it?" I asked.

"Uh-huh. I'm guessin' ya know what that means?"

"Yeah, I do. Did he say when he'll be back?"

"No."

"Can you make a guess when?"

"Maybe a coupla hours, I don't know. He was called out to a shooting. If it's straight forward, then he should be back soon. You wanna leave a message?"

"Yeah. Tell him I'll be in my office the rest of the day."

"That it?"

"Yeah, thanks. Oh, hold on. Let him know if he's back after six and still needs to talk to me, he can find me over on Nassau Street." I gave him a description of my car and plate number.

"You pullin' a stakeout or sumthin'?"

"Or something, yeah," I said.

There was a brief pause then, "Okay, got it."

"Thanks," I said then hung up.

'Christ', I thought as I hung up the phone. How the hell did they find out about me. This would seriously change how I would go on from here, especially as regards to my selfish wish to stay alive. It was definitely time to call for back-up. I picked up the phone again and dialed Elmore's number.

When he answered, I filled him in on where I was in my investigation and asked for his help. He agreed, as he always does.

Mind you, I had a few reservations about asking him specifically, namely because of his connections in the black community, notably, his possible ties to the black gangs, if any. I'd known El a long time and learned he wasn't a 'joiner' as such, but he was a proud black man, so there are certain sympathies.

I spent the rest of the afternoon busying myself with paperwork, mostly catching up on cases notes. I also used the time to put together some sort of plan in case I got lucky and could catch these guys out. Didn't take a lot planning actually. If I could catch them in act and get the drop on them, I would hook them up and call in the calvary, offering myself as a material witness. Sounded simple enough, I thought, but then I thought I heard a very soft chuckle at the back of my head. It felt like the gods that like to mess with my life every so often decided to take an interest.

Maggie came back at ten after two. She arrived carrying a fresh cup of coffee and set it on the desk, picking up the empty mug.

I looked up and watched her as she came in. It is always a pleasure to sit and watch her sometimes. Late twenties, five-foot and change, about one-ten. She had thick dark brown shoulder length hair that she always wore pulled back at the sides with a pair of ivory combs. She had a slender, but not overly thin, figure and always wore clothes that accentuated her narrow waist and perky breasts. But the best part, were her legs; long and perfectly proportioned like those of a ballet dancer.

Good thing I'm married to a woman who could outdo her.

"Glad to see you getting some of these files tidied up. I've been waiting on them so I can get the billing out," she said.

"Uh-huh," I said, snapping out of my reverie. I knew that she was always aware when I gave her the 'eye'. Happily, she never minded and knew that it was nothing more than admiration.

"So, does this mean this business about Gabe is over?"

"'Fraid not," I said. "Nothing I can do until tonight."

"Tonight? What's going on tonight?"

"Stakeout."

"Oh. By the way, did you call Silvano?" she asked.

I nodded. "Uh-huh. Wasn't in. He'll either call later or maybe hook up with me tonight."

"You think this'll take much longer?"

"Don't know, why? Something come in?"

"Sort of. A woman called, a Mrs. Edna Harding. She's looking for someone to find her daughter. Seems she ran away a few weeks ago and the mother thinks she's somewhere in the Village. She says that the daughter, Caroline, whose seventeen, by the way, was hanging around with some wild kids at her school."

"Lotta that going around these days," I said. "She been to the police?"

"Yeah, but no cheer."

"Where's she live?"

"Up in Scarborough. So, what do you want to do? Pass it over to Willie?"

William Burke was another private investigator I sometimes worked with whenever I needed help or had more work than I had time to handle. He's solid and reliable, in fact, I was thinking of bringing him in to help with the stakeout.

"No, not yet. He doesn't really know the Village that well. Call her back and tell her we'll take the case. See if she'll come in and bring anything that'll help find the girl. You know the drill: pictures, names of friends, boyfriend. You can start with the preliminaries. Make some calls. You know who. That okay with you?"

"Yeah, I can do that. This mean, I get a bonus," she said, smiling.

"Christ, woman. First, a raise, now a bloody bonus," I said, feigning being upset, then a moment later, smiling back. "Yeah. Same as always."

"Thanks, Murph. It'll come in handy."

"Huh?"

"Some detective," she said, patting her belly.

"No shit! When did you find out?" I asked.

"Today. That's where I was at lunchtime. Doctor thinks it will come maybe December, early January," she said, beaming.

"That's great news. Jane'll be over the moon when I tell her."

"Thanks."

Maggie turned and walked back to her desk. I was really happy about her news but now I had to think about how I was gonna replace her when the time came. Oh, well, that was a few months away. Maybe Abe would be on board with me by then.

I made one more call to Jane. I told her Maggie's news and, of course, she was thrilled and told me to tell she'd call her tomorrow. I also filled her in on my plans to start staking out the tavern tonight and to not expect me home until late. She said she would be okay, and for me to be careful, as usual and, just as usual, I said not to worry and that I would.

Detective Silvano called around ten to six. Maggie had left for the day, so I answered the phone.

"Murphy Confidential Investigations," I said.

"Burnin' the midnight oil?" Silvano said.

"More or less," I answered. "What's up?"

"Got some bad news for ya. Looks like some people been askin' 'round about you."

"Yeah, I sorta got that already."

"Whaddya mean? Somethin' happen?"

137

"Could say that. I spotted a tail today. He wasn't very good at it. Stood out like a sore thumb."

"And you think he's one of the guys you're after?"

"Better to think so, don't you think? Besides, I'm not working on anything else that would warrant a tail."

"Yeah, I 'spose so. Plus, it makes sense in light of recent developments."

"Do tell," I said.

"Looks like one of our uniforms might have an interest in what you're doin'. Somebody in the department happen to notice him in the squad room earlier today. He was nosin' through some of the files. Anyway, when I was told about it, I asked if he saw which files he was pokin' in. Care to take a guess?"

"Yours."

"Right. And sittin' right on top was the file I opened on your guys which included your name and address."

"Well, it couldn't last, staying anonymous, I mean. So, what did you do about the uniform?"

"Nothing direct. I figure if I keep him under surveillance for a day or two, maybe he'll lead me somewhere. If not, then I'll pull him in an' lean on him."

"So, how long this been going on?"

"Can't say. I seen him in and around the squad room a few times, but figured he was interested in gettin' into detective work.

Never figured him to be scoping out information."

"You think he's connected to the southerners over there?" I asked.

"Possible. Why else would he be snoopin' 'round the file you're connected with?"

"Makes sense, I suppose."

"So, you still thinkin' 'bout a stakeout?"

"Maybe."

"Ya know that if this guy passed this on his buddies, assumin' they are his buddies, then they'd be kind of stupid to keep hangin' out at the tavern, right?"

"Uh-huh, maybe. But, you hafta admit, they haven't exactly demonstrated a whole lot smarts so far," I said.

"No shit," Silvano said. "Listen, I passed your car and tag along to the night patrols with a heads up in case they spot you sittin' around an' get suspicious."

"Thanks. I'll give you a call tomorrow and let you know what happened tonight, if anything happens at all."

"Good 'nough. Watch your six, pal."

I hung up the phone and sat back thinking about all I had to go on. Silvano was probably right about one thing, it seemed unlikely that these guys would go back to Benny's. They had to know from the cop that was feeding them information, that a file was open now and that, even if they didn't know who they were specifically, they would be on the look out. So, if they've gone to ground the question was, where?

I reached for the phone and dialed.

"Silvano."

"It's me again. A quick question, when you guys fished that body out of the river, was there anything on it that would point to where he staying?"

"No. Only thing we found was that card with his name on it. There was some other stuff but the water sorta fucked them up beyond anythin' usable."

"Okay, thanks." I hung up. That would've been too easy.

A half hour later, I made a decision. I would forget the stakeout since it was likely to be a waste of time, and I'd rather be home anyway. Instead, I would head over to Kensington tomorrow and pay another visit to Maxie. This time I would press, hard if necessary.

I stood up and left, locking the office door behind me then headed upstairs.

* * *

At noon the next day, I was back in my car heading for Benny's place. The traffic was heavy as usual, but I managed to get there by one. I found a place to park and got out.

This time of day, the tavern was mostly empty except for a couple of barflies sitting in a corner nursing their beers. Maxie was sitting behind at a table at the far end of the room, reading a paper. When he looked up, I could see he remembered me.

"Lost agin?," he said, putting the paper down.

"Time for a talk Maxie," I said, stepping to the table and pulling a chair over.

"Whaddya mean, time ta talk?" he asked suspiciously. "Who are you? A cop, or sumthin'?"

"I think you know who I am. So save your breath and relax. This could be your lucky day, Maxie," I said, pushing my hat back on my head.

"Yeah? How so?" he asked, warily as he sat down.

"I'm not a cop. But If I don't like what you have to tell me, I can arrange for some pretty nasty ones I know real well to come and have the same talk. And, if that isn't enough, I know brothers who might be interested. I'm not here to fuck you up. I just want straight answers to a couple of questions. Got it?"

He nodded, starting to look nervous. "Yeah, got it."

"Okay, first question, what do you know about the guys been going around bracing the gays and hippies?"

"Nothin', man. Why'd I know anythin'?"

I saw that he was starting to look worried. I pressed on.

"Now you know that isn't the truth. Take a good look at me, Maxie. I can spot bullshit a mile away, so stop fucking with me. Talk."

He was sweating a little now.

"Man, you're fuckin' with my life here, ya know?"

"Yeah, well, that's what happens when you mix with bad people," I said, "so answer the question."

"Yeah...yeah, I 'eard sumthin' 'bout that but that's it, man. I ain't wantin' any trouble."

My first guess about him was right, spineless.

"So you're telling me you don't know any guys, southern guys, might be involved with any of this."

"Yeah, yeah, that's right. I don't know anybody like them."

"Now, you know, I don't believe you, right. Look. I can make these guys go away and maybe even send a little scratch your way if you tell me something I can use. All I want are their names and where I can lay my hands on them. Tell me that and I'm outta your life."

He sat thinking about his situation, weighing his options. After a brief moment, I saw the resignation suddenly come into his eyes.

"Yeah...yeah, okay," he said, leaning forward.

He proceeded to give me the names of two men and where there were staying. Turns out, their apartment was only a few blocks away which made sense. He also gave me more information on others and the connections between them. Seems it was a pretty loose community and only had about eight or ten active participants, some living at the same apartment building.

I pulled out my wallet, pulled out a fifty and slid it across the table.

"If I learn that you contacted these guys and warned them about me, the next visit will be from a couple of black friends of mine. Understood?" I said, standing up and looking down at him as he scooped up the bill.

"Yeah, no sweat. I'll keep my mouth shut, don't worry. I don't want any trouble."

I gave him a hard look then turned and headed back outside.

There was still plenty of time, so I decided to check out the address Maxie gave me.

It was located several blocks away on a short side street off of Wales Avenue.

It was a typical three storey apartment building. Five stone steps rose up to a double glass door. A small panel was set into the side wall on the right with six buttons next to little pieces of paper. I looked at these and saw only two names, my guys weren't there; must be leased to someone else, I thought.

I was about to head back to the sidewalk when a man stopped at the bottom and looked up at me.

"You lookin' fer somebody?" he asked in a surly tone when I stepped on the sidewalk. His southern accent heavy and thick.

"Yeah," I said. "Jake an' Bobby Lee. They told me this was where they lived."

"Y'all got the right place. They got a squat on the top floor. Whaddya want wit them?"

"I met them over at Benny's and they was tellin' me 'bout things. Thought I'd like to hear sum more," I said.

"Benny's, huh. Yeah, those boys is Klan through and through and they surely do like ta talk 'bout the Order, right enough. But iff'n y'all want ta hear more ya gotta come back later. They ain't usually 'round here much this time a day. Y'all have a better chance to git 'em at Benny's.

"Okay, thanks," I said and walked off.

Well, at least, now I knew where they were staying. I went back to my car. I checked my watch" almost two-thirty. I called it day and headed home.

* * *

Bobby Lee was dressed in jeans and a singlet. He walked barefoot to the stove and picked up a coffee pot sitting on the burner.

"Want one?' he asked, looking over his shoulder at Jake, who sat at the chrome table smoking a cigarette.

"Nah. Tell me agin what happened yesterday," he said.

"I tole ya, I wanted to find out who this guy was, so I looked him up in the phone book. I went over to where he had his office

144

and asked 'round for what he looked like then waited. He come out 'round noon an' I followed him but then lost him."

"That was stupid."

"Yeah? What would y'all have done, huh?" Bobby Lee said sitting down, sounding a bit miffed.

"Wouldn't've gone there in the first place."

"Yeah, well, that's you."

"You don't git it, do ya?"

"What?"

"The reason ya lost him was 'cause he made ya and probably followed y'all back here."

"No fuckin' way. Soon as I lost 'im, I split."

"Maybe," Jake said. He sat for a moment thinking, then said, "I think we gotta get outta here."

"Why?" Bobby Lee asked.

"In case this peeper knows where we are, that's why," Jake snapped. "By the way, ya said ya saw him. What'd he look like?"

Bobby Lee gave him a broad description of Murphy. Jake listened intently, interrupting him only a couple of times.

"I think I seen this guy before," he said when Bobby Lee finished.

"Huh? When? Where?"

"Benny's. The other day. A stranger came in when I was there waitin' on y'all to show up. Maxie said it was some salesman got lost."

"Shee-it. Y'all figurin' he maybe did KC?"
Jake shrugged.
"So, now what we gonna do?"
"Like I said, move. Call Jimmy. See iff'n he kin put us up."
"But that's right in the middle of all them faggots and freaks," Booby Lee said.
"So? It'd be the last place the peeper'd look."
"Maybe. Okay. I'll call 'im. By the way, how come ya figure he lives over there? Ya think he's one a them?" Bobby Lee asked, wiggling his hand as he went to the phone.
"Jimmy? Don't talk so crazy. I know'd him since we was kids back in the hills," Jake said.
A moment later, Bobby Lee said into the phone. "It's me, Bobby Lee."
"What's up?" Jimmy asked.
"Jake wants to know iff'n y'all kin put us up a while?"
"'The three of ya" Yeah, s'ppose so."
"Jus' the two of us. Me and Jake."
"Where's KC?"
"We'll fill ya in when we git there."
"Okay. When?"
He pulled the phone away from his ear and looked over at Jake.
"Wants ta know when?" he asked.
"Coupla hours," Jake said.
"Coupla hours," he repeated into the phone. "'Round six."
"Yeah, okay. See y'all then."

Chapter Eleven

The next morning I went down to the office long enough to check in with Maggie for an update on our new client. She had just about finished when the outer door opened, and two men came in. Both wore suits and fedoras, the standard uniform of wise guys and detectives. I was pretty sure they weren't wise guys, sooo...

"You Matt Murphy?" one of the men said. Maggie stood up and faced them.

"In the flesh. To what do I owe the pleasure of a visit from the TPD?" I said, smiling.

"I'm Detective Costello, this is Detective Jasper," the first man said, pulling out his shield, ignoring my comment.

I suppressed a smile, "Yeah? And?"

"We'd like you to accompany us to the station to answer a coupla questions," Costello said.

"About what?" I asked. "And, what station?"

"Downtown. You'll find out once we get there," Jasper put in.

"Headquarters? Kind of outta your area aren't you," I said.

"We got our reasons," Costello said.

"Uh-huh. Look why don't you guys pull up a seat and have a coffee and ask your questions here?"

"Sorry, just grab yer hat and let's go," Costello said.

Maggie had stayed where she stood while this exchange went on.

"Want me to call Phillip?" she asked as I stood up. Phillip Kennedy was the lawyer I sometimes used. He worked for the law firm that had me on retainer.

I looked at Costello, "Do I need a lawyer?"

"Not yet," he said, bluntly.

"No, don't bother...yet," I said to Maggie. Then, "Okay, let's go. My car or yours?"

"Ours," Jasper said. I decided that I didn't like Detective Jasper. Sour little shit. Obviously had no sense of humour.

"Before we go, you carryin'?" Costello asked.

I opened my jacket which I just happen to still have on showing my .38.

"I assume you got paper for that," he said.

"Yep. Wanna see?" I said.

"Never mind," he said.

A half hour later, we were in a windowless interview room at police headquarters. There was a single table and four wooden chairs sitting under a set of florescent lights that cast a harsh white light. I could only imagine the confessions that were obtained in here. They had given me a mug of coffee which sat on the empty table. I sat alone at the table. Jasper stood near the door leaning against the wall.

"Okay. You got me here, now what?"

"You know a place called, Benny's?" Costello asked, sitting down across from me and opening a file that he placed on the table.

"Yeah, but you already know that, right? I mean, if that's the file Detective Silvano opened then you know everything about what I'm doing and why, so let's cut to the chase and save everybody some time," I said, pointing at the file that he held.

"Okay. Look, I checked you out and from what I've been hearin' you're straight up. But I gotta ask ya some questions all the same."

"Yeah, sure, I understand. You got a job to do," I said, relenting a little.

"Good. Sometime late last night, four black men hit this Benny's. Really tore the place up and roughed up the bartender, a guy named Maxie," he said.

Okay, I thought. Now I knew where I stood and why I was here. Just then, the door opened, and Detective Silvano walked in, came over, and sat at the table next to Costello. We nodded to each other.

"Anyway, according to this Max, these black guys wanted to find the guys you're looking for."

"And this has what to do with me?" I asked.

"C'mon, Murphy, you know the answer to that. Did you sic these guys on the tavern?" Silvano said.

"No. Why would I? Like I told you before, the last thing I want to see happen is for a war to break out here. Besides, I'm not in touch with anyone in that community anymore."

"Yeah? Not even yer hoodlum buddy?" Jasper said from where he stood leaning against the wall.

"Yeah, not even him," I snapped.

"Look, we're in a spot here," Silvano said, cutting off any further exchange between Jasper and me. "According to Maxi you went to see him earlier and pressed him for information. Sez you threatened to tell your black friends about his place if he didn't tell you what you wanted to know. Is that true?"

"Yeah, it's true, so what? You knew I planned to go back to there since I've done my best to keep you posted. You never put a squeeze on someone to get information?" I said. "But I didn't contact anybody. Not my way of operating. If you talked to the people I think you did, then you'd know that already."

"So, how you figure these guys found out about the tavern?" Costello asked.

"All I can say about that is what I've read and heard about. These militant groups operating here have established networks of contacts they work with, some no doubt even into the TPD. These guys aren't stupid. It's also one of the reasons I'm purposely staying clear of any contact with my so-called, 'hoodlum buddy'," I said, casting a glance at Jasper.

"Okay, say we buy your story, and you were jus' leanin' on him. What'd he tell ya?" Costello asked.

"Not much. He gave me the names of two men: Jake Pickett and a Bobby Lee Crawford. He also gave me an address over on some side street off of Wales Avenue. And before you ask, yeah, I went there but they weren't home, so I left and headed home."

"That's it?"

"That's it. I was going to call Silvano and fill him in but you two showed up before I could."

"A real solid citizen," Jasper snickered.

"What the hell's your problem, pal? I do something to you?" I demanded, half rising from my chair.

"Take it easy, Murph, And you, go git a coffee," Costello said quickly to Jasper, who glared at me as he pushed himself off the wall, turned and left, slamming the door behind him.

"What the hell is his problem?" I asked again, sounding really pissed.

"Sorry, 'bout that. He's got some issues he's working on," Costello said.

"Yeah," Silvano added, "and we know you've been co-operatin', that ain't the problem. It's that Maxie kinda fingered you for leanin' on him, and Costello and Jasper took the call initially. I only heard about when I came in this morning,"

"That's right," Costello added. "We had to go through the drill 'cause it's been written up and the Watch Commander had a gander at it."

"That's okay, we're good. It's just that I don't like to be leaned on when it isn't called for," I said.

"So, you got anything else to share?" Silvano asked.

"Not really. I was planning on going back to the apartment building today and try to get something on these guys. According to one of the tenants I talked to, these guys are definitely Klan boys. Up here to stir up some shit and do a little recruiting."

"Look, I'm not tryin' to tell you your business but, like I said before, maybe you should back off and let us handle this. You're gettin' real close to interferin' with an ongoin' case here."

"Like I already told you, I can't and won't back off. As for interfering, that's not an issue."

"How'd ya figure that?" Costello asked.

"I know the guys at Village station are looking into the muggings, I get that, but I'm not. My interest is to find the guys that attacked a friend of mine and put him in the hospital. It just so happens that it coincides with your investigation which is why I'm even talking to you guys in the first place."

The two detectives sat looking at me for a moment. Finally, Costello stood up and Silvano closed the file.

"Okay. We're done here. For now. Just watch your step and keep in touch," Costello said then turned and exited the room.

"Thanks. Any chance of a ride back to my office?" I asked, standing up.

"Yeah," Silvano said. "I'll get a patrol car to run you back."

"Thanks."

We left the room together. I followed him back to his desk. Jasper wasn't anywhere in the squad room which didn't upset me any.

"So, what's Jasper's story? He seemed to go out of the way to ride me?" I asked when we arrived at his desk.

"Huh? Oh, he's dealin' with some bad personal shit right now. Marriage is breaking up. Plus, he jus' learned he didn't pass his Sergeants test."

"Tough. Life's not always an easy ride, but you gotta learn to carry whatever crap it throws at you and not lay it on everybody else," I said.

"I know. He'll work it out. He's a good man and cop," he said, reaching for the phone on his desk.

A moment later, he said that a car was waiting downstairs to take me back to the Village. I said I would keep in touch as we shook hands then left.

A half hour later, I was back in the office.

"So, what was that all about?" Maggie asked when I stepped past the door.

"Just routine. Seems Benny's got hit last night and the bartender dropped my name. Any chance of a coffee?" I said, heading for my office.

"Yeah, sure," she said, getting up. "And then what?"

"Nothing. They know about my connection to El and that he gave me a head's up about some brothers on the prowl for whoever killed the black man the other night. They had the idea that maybe I gave El the name of the tavern, and he passed it on to one of the brothers," I said as she followed me into the office carrying my coffee.

"So are they going to keep after you?"

"Probably not."

"Okay. Now what?"

"I'll drive back over and check out the apartment building again."

"Think that's wise?" she asked.

"Probably not, but I have to find out where they are so I can get what I need to finish this. Enough of that, what you got for me since I was gone?"

"Not much. I called the hospital. Gabe's doing really great. Figures to be released sometime next week."

"Great. What about this new case? Anything?"

She shook her head.

"Talked with the mother and got the information you wanted. She said her daughter had been hanging out with three friends from school, two girls and a boy. I got their names. Seems all of them took off at the same time. Apparently, there isn't a steady boyfriend that she's aware of. She's coming in tomorrow with pictures and other items."

"Okay, thanks. Great work. What time she due?" I asked.

"Around three," Maggie said.

"Okay. I'll try and be here. That everything?"

"Uh-huh."

I checked my watch: almost three.

"If you haven't got anything else pressing to do, why don't you pack up and go home. I'll be hanging in here for a bit before heading off."

"Okay, thanks. That'll give me time for a little bit of shopping," she said, smiling.

"See ya tomorrow."

At three o'clock, I closed up the office and headed for the hospital to look in on Gabe then swung by for a quick visit with Manny Rodriquez.

"Hey, what's up?" I said as I approached Manny's desk. He looked a little distracted.

"Heard about what happened at Benny's an' your visit with Costello and Jasper. A bit rough?"

"Could say that, yeah," I said, sitting down. "How'd...?"

"Gus told me. They called him first thing this morning, Checkin' you out; I'm guessin' just before paying you a visit."

I gave him the Reader's Digest version of my meeting with Costello.

"So what brings you here?"

"I don't know if they filled you in, so I thought I'd stop by and update you," I said.

"Okay, so update."

Five minutes later, I had finished filling him in on everything I learned to date and my plan to head back over to Kensington from here.

"Think that's smart, given that they know 'bout you now?' Manny asked.

"Don't matter if it's smart or not."

"Hmm. You're one stubborn gringo, pal. I respect why you're doin' it but, shit, man."

"Yeah."

"Okay. Jus' watch yer butt. Silvano know you're goin' back?'"

"Yeah," I said, nodding. "You got anything new?"

"Yeah. Looks like there's been a coupla incidents last night. Mostly jus' some pushin' and yellin'. Beat cops were able to handle it. No arrests."

"Where?"

"The Park area. 'Cordin' to the reports, one of the attackers had a heavy southern accent."

"Interesting. Sound like my guys?"

"Don't think so. Uniform's notes don't jibe with what you gave us on your guys."

"Shit. That means there's more of them working the Village. This could develop into a real problem, especially if they start targeting any more blacks.”

“We know.”

“For what it's worth, I think that one, or both, of the guys I'm looking for might be the ringleaders.”

“Hmm. Thanks, I'll make a note.”

“Okay. I'm off. Say hi to Gus for me,” I said, standing up.

“Keep in touch.”

Back in the parking lot, I climbed into my car and headed for Kensington.

I made it to Marshall Street in good time. It was still an hour or so before the daylight would be gone. I parked and, after checking my gun, got out and headed for the apartment building.

As I walked towards the front door of the apartment building, I thought about how I was going to approach this. I decided the best way was to just go straight ahead, no subtlety. I entered the foyer and headed up the stairs. It was dead quiet. When I reached the third floor, I went to the apartment door and placed my ear against the door. Nothing.

I tried the door. It was unlocked. Uh-oh, I thought, easing my gun out. Crouching down, I turned the knob and slowly pushed the door open.

The apartment was empty. It was a simple one bedroom with a small toilet opposite the door. The bedroom was located just to the right of the toilet. I spotted an unmade double bed. Guess they didn't have an issues with bunking together, considering. The living room and kitchen made up the main room. Nothing but tacky dated furniture filled the apartment. Shit, I thought, even the Sally Anne wouldn't take this stuff.

I stepped inside and closed the door, re-holstering my gun. I spotted several cups and dishes still on the chrome table. A kettle sat on the two-burner electric range. It was stone cold. Looked like they left in a bit of a hurry. There were newspapers scattered around the living room and on the table. The coffee table was littered with several empty beer bottles, two ashtrays filled with stubbed out butts and bits of papers.

Ten minutes later, I had finished a sweep of the apartment. I found several pamphlets and leaflets selling the Klan message but not much else. The only other item was a hand-written piece of paper with a phone number on it by the phone. I recognized it as being for the Queen's Park area. I had a gut feeling that they split, but why, and where did they go? I looked down at the phone number. Could they have gone to the Park? If they did, what for?, I mean, if they hated the gays so much why would they move over there where they hung out? Well, I thought, like I said, they haven't been showing a lot of smarts so far.

I finished up and left. I drove over to the 6th for a quick visit with Manny. Maybe he could use his resources and see if he could get me an address for the phone number.

Chapter Twelve

The Chevy pulled into an alley and moved toward the rear of the building. Jake and Bobby Lee exited the car. Jake paused long enough to pull the small Confederate flag from the aerial, no sense in advertising their presence, then the two went to the back door of the four-story building.

Jimmy Dixon was from the same county back home as KC, Jake, and Bobby Lee. In fact, he was KC's cousin. He was tall and lanky standing six-four. One would never guess that he was in his early forties judging by his baby face looks which made him look more like late twenties, early thirties. He had come north about a year ago after two of the mines back home closed down. He managed to get hired on as a truck driver for a local delivery company. Dixon was a life-time member of the Klan, indoctrinated from boyhood.

"So, what's up?" Jimmy Dixon asked when he opened the door and let them inside.

"We got some heat on our assess an' need a place to lay low," Jake said, dropping a bag he'd taken with him on the floor.

"Heat? Ya mean, cops?"

Jake shook his head and said, "Naw. Some private dick been nosin' 'round."

"What the hell's a private dick doin' pokin' inta our business?" Jimmy pressed when he closed the door and followed the two men into the room.

"He's 'spposed ta be a friend of some queer we roughed up a few nights back," Bobby Lee answered. "Hey, y'all got any cold beer in this place?"

"In the fridge," Jimmy said. "Yeah, I heard 'bout that. So it was y'all that did him. I guess it was y'all that did that ole nigger too, huh?"

"Bring me one to," Jake said as Bobby Lee went into the kitchen. "Yeah, that was us."

"So, where's KC?" Jimmy asked.

"Dead," Jake said.

"Whaddya mean, dead? How? Who...?"

"Shot. We think it was summa them niggers from Kensington. Fished him outta the Don," Bobby Lee said, coming back carrying three bottles of beer.

"Jee-sus H Christ," Jimmy said, sitting down. "And the cops...?"

"Don't know. All I know is they don't seem to have connected him to us," Jake said.

"What about this detective fella? He a problem?"

"Maybe," Bobby Lee said.

"Bobby Lee here tracked 'im down to a place over on Spadina. Went and staked out the place," Jake said.

"Yeah, and?" Jimmy asked.

Jake cast a look at Bobby Lee.

"I fucked up. He made me," he said.

"He made you? You mean he followed you back to the squat?"

"Don't think so, but we figured we better not take the chance and split," Jake put in.

"You reckon he's gone to the cops?"

"Looks that way."

"So the cops is lookin' for y'all?" Jimmy asked, a note of alarm in his voice.

"Naw. We'd a got word from Maxie's cop contact."

"Hmm. Whadda 'bout that queer you put in the hospital? Think he kin identify any a you?"

"Don't think so. It was dark an' we was on him mighty quick. 'Sides, you know what they're like, scared shitless."

"Maybe. But looks like his buddy ain't." Jimmy paced the room thinking, then said, "Okay. We better deal with this situation quick. First thing is the queer. He knows somethin' for sure, else how'd he put this dick onta y'all. If this guy manages to connect us all could be a shit load of trouble we don't need. You boys bring yer hardware with you?"

Both men nodded.

"What ya got in mind? Kill 'im?" Bobby Lee asked.

"Not yet. Let me dwell on it a spell. I'll let ya know later," Jimmy said.

"So, now what'll we do in the meantime?" Bobby Lee asked.

"Git y'all set up in some new digs," Jimmy said.

"Good."

"I got word them black fuckers are lookin' for the ones did that ole man. Way I hear it, sum one tole them it was us boys that did it, so they on the hunt for any southerners," Jimmy said.

"Yeah, that's what we heard too," Jake said.

"Okay. The first thing I gotta do is git you boys sum place where you kin hole up. You figure it's safe for y'all to be on the streets?"

"Yeah, I reckon so," Jake said. "We got away clean. Nobody knows 'bout you, or where we mighta went."

"Good," Jimmy said, getting up and going to a small desk where he scribbled something a piece of paper.

When he came back, he gave it to Jake. "Go to this address down in Little Italy and ask for Roscoe. He's a member an' will set y'all up with a new squat. Should be safe for a while. He's with them bikers, Satan's Choice."

Jake took the piece of paper and looked at it.

"Try'n stay low for a bit. No sense makin' it easy for the bastards to find ya."

Jake and Bobby Lee finished off their beers and then picked up their bags and headed back the car.

"Okay. Here's what we'll do. We keep up our recruitin'. Git the word out," he said.

"Yeah sure, but whatta 'bout what Jimmie said 'bout stayin' low?" Bobby Lee asked. He really liked kicking the crap out of these guys. "An' whatta 'bout that peeper fella? You got any ideas what to do 'bout him?"

"Yeah. Bobby Lee...we set him up an' take him out an' dump the body in the lake. You better start packin' yer piece jus' in case y'all meet up wit him or them niggers."

"Way ahead a ya," Bobby Lee said, opening his jacket showing a .38 Smith and Weston tucked in the waist of his pants.

"Okay. We gotta do this right, hear. We don't know how well he's connected. Plus, we don't wanna bring the cops down on us."

"No sweat," Bobby Lee said, calmly. "It ain't like we ain't done this before."

"Uh-huh, but this ain't back home. We got no one watchin' our backs. So, y'all jus' make sure ya do this up right."

"Okay. Git to it."

* * *

Manny Rodriquez was sitting at his desk with his head buried in a file when I arrived. I knew him well enough to know that he wasn't big on paperwork. Most of the good detectives weren't, preferring to be out there, solving crime, and busting the perpetrators. But, as they say, paper is the lifeblood of any bureaucracy, and the Toronto Police Department could be as bureaucratic as any area of politics. It was a big reason why I quit the force way back when.

"Buy you a coffee?" I said, pulling a chair over and sitting down.

He looked up. He looked tired.

"Like to, but can't," he said, without smiling. "Thanks anyway. So, why ya here? Got somethin'?"

"Not really. I just got back from Little Italy. I paid a visit to the apartment building where these guys had a squat. Looks like they've split."

"Think they left the city and gone back home?"

"Don't know. I'm kind of leaning to no but can't be sure."

"Go on," he said.

"I found a couple of things that I think suggest that they haven't," I said, pulling out the pamphlets and leaflets I found and passed them over to him. He quickly thumbed through them.

"I'd say these guys might be part of some kind of recruiting effort the Klan's working. In fact, I think these guys might be running the show."

"Hmm, yeah, maybe. We been pickin' up some news from the street 'bout some people trying to stir up shit against the gays and blacks. 'Specially over in the Park area an' in some of the gay bars. They certainly picked the right time to push their line of horseshit with all this unrest goin' on."

"What about that special squad run by the Feds? They getting anything they're willing to share?"

"Yeah, right! Like that'll happen any day soon," Manny said.

"Just thought I'd ask," I said. "Look. Can you do me a favour and run this phone number for me and get an address?"

I pulled out the piece of paper with the number on it and passed it over to him.

"Where'd ya get it?" he asked, looking at it.

"From the apartment."

"Yeah, okay. Leave it with me. Call me in a coupla hours."

"Okay, thanks," I said, standing up.

"Where ya goin' now?"

"Home. I'll call you from there."

"Okay. See ya."

Later, I called Manny. He had the information I needed. The number was assigned to a man named, Jim Dixon. He lived in an apartment building on Manning Avenue about a block away from Christie Pits Park; Freddie Giovanni's backyard. I decided I would head over there tomorrow for another chat with him.

Tonight I would stay in and enjoy the benefits of married life.

I went down to the office around nine-thirty, carrying a plate with two fresh Danish pastries Jane made the day before. Maggie was at her usual spot. She had a small addiction for pastry, especially Danish, and if shewas anything like Jane was when she was pregnant, then her appetites were going to go wacky.

"Mornin'," I said when I stepped inside.

"Morning," she said, eyeing the plate in my hand. "Is that what I think it is?"

"Yep." I walked past her desk to the coffee machine and poured a cup.

"Stop teasing, Murph," she said, a hint of mock hurt in her voice.

"Yeah, okay. It isn't as much fun as used to be," I said, setting the plate down on her desk. She smiled like a little girl on Christmas morning.

"When you finish stuffing yourself, come inside and bring me up to date," I said, smiling.

Ten minutes later, she opened the door and came in with a file and her notebook.

"Happy?"

"What do you think," she said smiling. She sat on one of the two chairs in front of my desk.

"Good," I said. "Shoot."

"Nothing much going on. I'm still digging into that missing girl case that just came in. Made some calls around like you suggested. So far, nothing. Said they'd call if they find out anything. By the way, you still planning on being here when the mother comes in later today?"

"Yeah. What time did you say she was coming in?"

"Around three," she said.

"Okay, thanks. Anything else?"

"Not much. Just the usual stuff. I can handle it. Oh, yeah, Abe called. He said it wasn't important. How about you? Making any progress?"

I nodded. "Yeah, some. I got a handle on the guys that hurt Gabe. Looks like they left the Market and have maybe moved into the Little Italy area somewhere."

"Isn't that 'Fingers' turf?"

I nodded.

"Does that mean you know where they are?"

"I got an idea."

"I'm curious. If you know who they are, and maybe where they are, then why haven't you turned everything over to Manny?"

"Wouldn't do any good. It's not enough for the cops to take action."

She gave me a funny look.

"I know they're the ones and, maybe I can convince Manny they're the ones, but without solid evidence he can't arrest them. He can't even haul them in for a line up."

"Not even if Gabe gave him a description?"

"Not enough."

"So how do you get the evidence?"

"Best way would be to catch them in the act."

"Isn't that kind of dangerous?"

"I suppose so, but I'm not so easy to brush off."

"I know, Matt, but you have obligations now, you know, and...," she started to say.

"I know, baby. But these guys aren't that bright or dangerous, really," I said, trying to reassure her.

"I understand that, but dumb doesn't necessarily mean stupid and sometimes they are as lucky as the smart."

"Wow! You been saving that up for just the right moment?" I said, chuckling.

"Yeah, I guess it did sound sorta silly, didn't it?" she said, blushing slightly.

"Actually, no. Thanks for worrying, but believe me I can handle this."

"I know."

"Okay. If that's it, then get outta here and let me call Abe."

She stood up and headed back to her desk. As I watched her leave, I felt glad that she was part of my operation.

I reached for the phone and dialed.

"Goldman."

"Hey. It's me. You called? What's up?" I said into the mouthpiece.

"Nothing, just wanted to get caught up on the case," Abe said.

"Not much. I know who the guys are that attacked Gabe and located where they've been staying. Went over and checked it out but got there too late.”

“Why too late?”

“Looks like they split. They might've moved to new digs around Little Italy.”

“This keeps up you should think about opening a branch office.”

“Gee, never thought of that,” I said sarcastically. “Maybe I should and hire you to run it. Whaddya think?”

The line went quiet for several moments.

“Hey, I was just kidding,” I said.

“Anyway, why do you think these guys have moved over there?” Abe asked, speaking again.

“Looks like the Klan might be trying to get a foothold up here. More likely, I'm thinking that is just a front for some of their more sinister activities.”

“Christ almighty. You ever think we'd be having this kind of conversation? The Klan in the Village. Sounds like a contradiction.”

“I know,” I said.

“I'm glad I'm packin' it in,” he said. “Everything's goin' to hell in a hand basket.”

“First time I ever heard you sound so fed up, buddy. So I guess you're making the right call then.”

“Yeah, I think so. Time to leave to it someone younger. Someone less used up.”

“I wouldn't go that far.”

“Yeah. Guess you're right. Anyway, Millie and I talked it over, you know, your offer. If it's still on the table let's talk when we get back."

"Hey, that's great, Abe. I'll work out some paperwork outlining everything and have it ready when you get back."

"Okay, and Matt...thanks," Abe said.

"Not necessary, pal. I'm looking forward to it," I said, smiling.

"Let's get together on the weekend and celebrate, up for it?"

"You bet. I'll let Jane know and she and Millie can work out the details."

"As if we had a chance of that not happening," he said, chuckling.

"Ain't marriage great. Talk later," I said then hung up.

* * *

Jake and Bobby Lee sat in the front of the Chevy. Jake was behind the wheel. He pulled a pack of Camels from his shirt pocket and tapped it against the side of his hand, dislodging a couple of cigarettes. He raised the pack to his lips and pulled a cigarette out then reached across to Bobby Lee, offering him one.

"Whaddya think?" Bobby Lee asked, reaching for a cigarette.

"'Bout?" Jake asked as he flipped open the Zippo.

"Jimmy's plans."

Jake shrugged, returning the cigarettes to his pocket. "Heard 'em before."

"Yeah, I know, but I mean 'bout what he said 'bout dealin' wit that PI and them niggers."

"I ain't gotta problem wit any a that," he said. "We jus' do em same as we'd do it back home."

"Yeah, I git that, but this ain't back home. Up here they fight back. Look at what they did to KC."

"Don't matter none. We do what we gotta do," Jake said, turning the key and firing up the engine that rumbled to life.

"So, now what?" Bobby Lee asked.

"I wanna go check out this Murphy's place. See what we kin git on him then take 'im out."

He slipped the car into gear, eased out the clutch and headed for the street.

Twenty minutes later he driving up Spadina Street.

"There," Bobby Lee said, pointing to the house that had a small sign nailed beside the door.

Jake pulled over to the curb half a block down from the building.

"Now what?" Bobby Lee asked.

"Don't know yet, I'm thinkin'," Jake said. "You said y'all seen him, right?"

Bobby Lee nodded, "Uh-huh."

"So y'all would spot him agin, yeah?"

"Yeah, so?"

Jake didn't answer right away. "Let me think."

"Ya want me to try and tail him agin?"

"Naw. He'd only make y'all agin. I think maybe we see if we kin figure out where he goes, maybe where he lives, an' take him there. Funny place to run a business outta."

"Huh?"

"A house. It's a funny place to run a business like his from."

"Yer right. I'd never wudda thought a that. How ya figurin' on takin' him down?"

"Don't know yet." Then after a moment, he said, "Maybe Jimmy's got some people we kin talk ta, you know, from them he's recruited, or that biker, Roscoe. I hear them Satan Choice dudes are badass. Could be they know sumthin' or kin get what we need."

"Yeah, that would work. You wanna ask 'im?"

Jake shook his head. "Naw, not yet. I wanna see iff'n we kin locate what hospital that queer is in."

"Why?"

"I figure he's the one put this Murphy on to us, which means he can also put the cops on to us. We git him first and then take care of this guy."

"Okay, sounds good," Bobby Lee said.

They headed to a bar where one of their friends from back home frequented. His name was Jesse Boggs and he has been living here for the last two years. He was also a full pledged member of their Order.

When they went inside the bar, they saw him sitting near the back talking to a couple of men. Jake and Bobby Lee made there way across the room.

"Damn, boy," a man said from one of the tables, as they passed by, "that you, Bobby Lee Crawford?"

"Gaw-damn. Cletus? What the fuck y'all doin' here?" Bobby Lee said accepting the other's outstretched hand. "When'd y'all git here?"

"Two days ago. They shut down number twelve last month. Over fifty good men outta work wit nothin'. Ain't no work back home, so I figure, what the fuck, head up here see iff'n I kin git any work here. My ole man knows ole Jesse there and makes a call. Jesse's settin' sumthin' up for me."

"Damn, boy. Sure good to see y'all. So things are bad back home?"

"Yeah. Everybody's hurtin'. A lot don't know what they gonna do."

"Shee-it, ain't nothin' we ain't used to," Bobby Lee said. "Hey. This here is Jake Pickett. We been runnin' together a while. He's from Grover's County."

"Hey," Cletus said, offering his hand which Jake shook. "I heard sum 'bout you. Nice ta meet y'all."

"You too," Jake said. "Whatcha been hearin'?"

"You're okay."

Jake just nodded indicating that he understood.

Just then, Jesse Boggs stepped up to them. "See you boys know each other," he said.

"Yeah. Cletus here is a second cousin on my Ma's side," Bobby Lee said.

"That's great," Jesse said. "Leave off the family reunion for now, okay. I got sumthin' I need to talk to you boys about. You don't mind, do ya Clet?"

"No, man. Y'all git to what ya gotta do. I'll catch up later. See y'all," he said, turning back to the other man at the table.

"What's up?" Jake asked, as they followed Jesse to the back of the room where the two men he was talking with stood waiting.

"I got a coupla guys I want y'all to meet. This is Mike Follett and Kevin James," Jesse said, introducing them.

"A coupla new members joined up a few months back. They're longtime residents here in the Village and don't like what's been happenin' lately wit all these freaks and queers takin' over everywhere."

"Yeah, we kin understand how y'all would be unhappy," Bobby Lee said.

"They been really useful gittin' our message out there, iff'n you git my meanin'. Jimmy called me an' filled me in. I was thinkin' that maybe these guys would be useful in helpin' wit your problem."

"How so?" Jake said.

"First, they're connected throughout the Village and kin find out most anythin'. Next, they're willin' to whatever needs doin'. They said they'd be happy to work wit us, so I asked them to hook up wit you two to help git this business taken care of."

"Funny," Jake said. "Me an' Bobby Lee was jus' sayin' we oughta find us a coupla boys what know the lay of this place ta hep out."

"Good. I'll leave y'all alone to git tho know each other," Jesee said, looking at him and giving a quick nod.

"Okay."

"Let's grab us a coupla chairs an' sit." They all pulled up chairs and sat down.

"So? What y'all know so far?" Jake asked the two men after Jesse left.

Jake and Bobby Lee sat and listened while the one named Mike filled them in on what they knew. It turned out that Jimmy pretty much filled them in on everything. These guys must be alright if Jimmy confided so much to them, Jake thought, when they finished talking.

"So, tell us what ya need," Mike Follett said.

"A coupla things," Jake said. "First, we need to know the hospital where that queer is at. Next, we need anything y'all kin git on this PI, Murphy. He's our biggest problem."

"Yeah, okay. Murphy, you say?" Follett said, looking at Kevin James. "Didn't we hear somethin' about that guy a while ago?"

"Yeah, come ta think about it, yer right. As I remember it, he was a friend of that piece of shit Crazy Pete. Ya remember him, he was da one that did me outta a coupla hundred bucks in that pool hall. A real hustler."

"Oh yeah, I remember. But ain't he dead or something?"

"Yeah, some college kid did him. Anyway, it was this Murphy went after the killer. Suppose ta be a real hard case. Ain't afraid to waste anyone either, from what I hear. Think I heard he's the one took out Mitchel and Tate. Likes the darkies and fags too."

"Yeah, yeah, now I remember," Follett said, turning back to Jake. "This guy ain't gonna be an easy hit or pushover. He's tough and got some juice and connections as I recall."

"Yeah, well, we'll jus' hafta deal wit that when we gotta," Bobby Lee, piped in.

"Okay. All good to know. For now, kin you find where the fag is?"

"Yeah, no problem. In fact, I'd bet he's over in Mount Sinai. If he's a Jew that'd be where they'd've taken him."

"Check it out and make sure an' let us know," Jake said. "I think for now, we should hook up here when we need to meet. Here's where y'all kin contact me or Bobby Lee," Jake said, giving him a phone number. "If you cain't reach us quick like, then call Jimmy."

Mike took the number and put it in his shirt pocket. Then, he and Kevin stood up and, after a quick handshake, headed for the door.

"So, whaddya think?" Bobby Lee asked once they were out of earshot.

"Looks like they'll do. 'Sides, Jimmy seems to be cool wit them."

"I don't like what they'all said 'bout that Murphy fella. Looks like he could be a lot harder to deal wit than we thought."

"Hmm, yeah, I know," Jake said. "Let's wait and deal the queer first."

Chapter Thirteen

The weekend was creeping up on me and I still didn't have enough to nail the bastards. Seems they decided to go to ground and curtail their late-night activities.

The meeting with Mrs. Harding, our new client, went as expected. Maggie had done an A1 job of getting information. So far, we hadn't actually located her daughter but we were able to calm her fears a little.

I explained to her that there were a lot of young people showing up in Yorkville these days. Many attracted by the new counterculture movement, some just for the excitement of the place.

She said she couldn't understand why her daughter would be running away. Like most parents, she thought the girl was happy and everything was okay. I told her that it wan't a reflection on her but simply the way things were now. The world seemed to be more accessible; everything was changing, which added to the allure to break away from the old ways with many kids hitchhiking their way across the country to places like the Village and Vancouver in search of whatever was the hip thing. Old Jack Kerouac would be proud, I thought.

She said she understood what I was telling her, but I could see that she was confused and hurt that it could have happened with her daughter.

"All I want is to know that she's okay," she said when I finished.

"We'll do the best we can to get you that assurance, but you have to understand, we can't force her to go home."

"I see."

"And you should be prepared for the possibility that Caroline won't want you to know where she staying."

Mrs. Harding choked back a sob and nodded.

"It may not help, but generally, most of these kids return home when they're ready."

She nodded, again. "It just that I've heard such horrible stories of what can happen here, especially to young girls."

"I won't lie to you. The Village has a dark side, but mostly it's not such a bad place and most of the people who live here are good people."

"Thank you. I'll just have to hope and pray you find her and she's okay, I guess."

We finished the meeting about ten minutes later and Mrs. Harding left after paying another two hundred dollars to cover another couple of days of looking.

"Poor woman," Maggie said.

"These cases are never easy on the parents," I said.

"So, you going to take over?"

"No. You got a good handle on it, so keep at it. Good job so far, by the way."

"Thanks. I got a couple of leads I'm still looking into," she said, smiling.

"Keep me updated. If you need my input let me know."

"Okay."

An hour later Maggie buzzed a phone call through to me.

"Murphy," I said when I picked up.

"It's me, Ed."

"What's up?" I asked.

"One a da boys came in a while ago said that he heard that there's a couple yokels nosin' aroun' lookin' for anythin' on ya."

"Really? He say who they were? Did they sound like southerners?"

"No," Ed said.

"Can you ask him and let me know?"

"He's here now if ya wanna to talk ta him direct."

"Put him on," I said.

Ed called out, 'Hey Norm. C'mere.'

"Yeah?" a man said into the phone.

"Your name is Norm?" I said.

"Yeah, who's dis?"

"I'm Matt Murphy. Ed says you heard that there're some people looking for me?"

"Yeah, maybe. Don't know if they was lookin' for ya but they was askin' a lot a questions 'bout who you was."

"Were they southerners?"

"Naw. Sounded more like they from over 'round Scarborough, ya know, like they was educated if ya get me."

"What kind of things were they wanting to know?"

"Usual stuff, I 'spose. Where ya hang out. Where ya live. Who ya know, shit like that."

"Anything else? You get a name on these guys?"

"Naw. But one a my buddies thinks he's seen 'em down 'round the Park, hangin' 'round wit some assholes pushin' a line of crap against the queers and blacks."

"Okay, thanks. By the way, you get a description on these guys?"

He didn't have a definitive description but did give me enough that I thought I might be able to spot at least one of them. I asked him to put Ed back on.

"Thanks for the call. Do me a favor and stand Norm to a few beers for me and I'll be by later to square with you, okay?"

"Sure, no sweat. Glad I was able to help. I get anythin' else, I'll call. See ya when I see ya," he said, then hung up.

Great, I thought, now I got something else to watch out for, as if I didn't have enough already. I decided it was time to take this head on.

A few hours later, Maggie buzzed me again saying that there was a Doctor Mathews from Mount Sinai on the line wanting to speak to me.

"Doctor," I said when she put the call through. "Is everything alright with Gabe?"

"Mr. Murphy. Yes, yes, he's doing very well. That's not why I'm calling. I saw a note on his file that said you were to be contacted if anything happened."

"Uh-huh. I take it something has happened?"

"I don't know if it is important, but I thought it was odd enough that I should call you."

"Okay, shoot," I said.

"Well, a few hours ago there was a strange man snooping around the ward. When the duty nurse asked him what he was looking for he said he was looking for his friend."

"That doesn't sound odd to me," i said.

"True, but when she asked for this friend's name, the man just turned and left."

"Hmm, now that is interesting. Do you think it'd be okay to come by and talk with her?"

"Yes. She'll be on duty today until midnight. You can come anytime. Her name is Kathy Williams, I'll let her know you'll be stopping by."

"Thanks. I'll be over within the hour. And, thanks too, for calling."

"No problem. I hope it's nothing serious."

"Me too," I said then hung up.

I grabbed my jacket and hat and stepped in to the outer office.

"What's up?" Maggie asked, looking a bit worried. "Is everything okay with Gabe?"

"Yeah, he's good. But something came up and I have to go over there and talk with a nurse. I'll check in later."

"Okay. Be careful."

I arrived at the hospital forty-five minutes later and headed straight up to the second floor. I found Nurse Williams sitting at her station pouring over what I assumed were patient files.

She was dressed in the traditional white uniform: knee length dress with her nursing pin on a lapel, white stockings and shoes with the two-inch block heel and a nurse's cap with a thick black band on it.

I guessed her to be in her early thirties. She had thick shoulder length light brown hair tied up in a bob and sticking out from under the cap at the back. She looked to be about five-five or so with a very attractive figure and pretty face. Another quick glance showed a plain gold band on the third finger of her left hand. Hey, I am a trained detective, after all.

"Mrs. Williams?" I said, as I approached the counter that enclosed her station.

"Yes. Can I help you?" she replied, looking up at me smiling.

"My name's Matt Murphy. I understand you're expecting me."

"Oh, yes. Dr. Mathews said you would be by. How can I help you?"

"Is there someplace we can go and talk for a few minutes?"

"Yes, of course," she said, standing up.

Turning to face an open door behind her, she call out, "Mary?"

A moment later a young nurse stepped in the doorway.

"Yes?" she said.

"Can you watch the desk for few minutes, please. I have to have a chat with this gentleman."

"Of course," Mary said as she came over and sat down at the desk.

"Thanks. I'll only be about five minutes or so." Then turning, she stepped past me saying, "This way, please."

She led the way down the hall to an empty room with a table and several chairs in it. I do so enjoy following behind a woman, especially when she looks as good as this one.

"Would you care for a cup of coffee?" she offered once we were in the room.

"Thanks, no. I don't want to keep you any longer than necessary," I said, pulling out a chair for her.

"Thank you," she said, sitting down. "As I understand it, you want to know about that man that was here earlier?"

"That's right," I said, sitting down.

"I don't know how much I can tell you. He wasn't really here all that long."

"But there was something about him that made you suspicious."

"Well, maybe, not suspicious, exactly. But he was definitely acting a bit, um, odd."

"Odd? How?"

"I don't know. I think it was the way he seemed lost, or perhaps uncertain about what he was doing here. I know it sounds silly."

"Not at all," I said, smiling. "It just means you have good instincts."

She smiled and almost blushed. "Thank you. After a while on this job, one does kind of get a sense about people. We deal with so many at the most vulnerable time in their lives, you know, when they drop a lot of their safeguards out of concern and worry and fear for those they care about."

"Sounds like an exhausting job," I said.

"Sometimes, but I'm lucky."

I must have had a quizzical look because she said, "My husband."

"Ah. Yeah, it's good to have someone to go home to for sure."

"Well, you're not here for that, so, what would you like know?"

"I think it would be best if you could just go over everything you remember about this man. You know, his demeanour, description, those sort of things. And don't worry if you think it too trivial, just tell me everything, okay?" I said, taking my notebook out.

She nodded then started to give me a complete account of that meeting with the man. I took notes as she told her story. She finished several minutes later.

From what she said, I was able to confirm that the man wasn't one of the two guys I was after. She did give me a very good description of the man, however. Forties. Two hundred plus pounds. Six-foot. She thought that his nose had been broken at some time. He looked like he did a lot of physical labour.

"That's about it," she said. "Like I said, it wasn't anything in particular that caught my attention, except maybe his leaving when I asked for his friend's name."

"Thanks," I said, closing my notebook and putting back inside my jacket pocket. "You've been a great help."

"Really? I didn't think I had anything to give you," she said, standing up.

"You'd be surprised what people really know but aren't aware of," I said. "By the way, is there a phone I could use?"

"Yes. Just there in the corner. Dial 'O' for the switchboard."

"Thanks. How's Gabe been doing," I asked as I stepped to the phone.

"Oh, he's a delightful man. Not many would be so uplifting after what happened to him."

"Yeah, he's a charmer for sure."

Nurse Williams smiled and then left me alone. I picked up the phone and dialed 'O'. When the operator came on the line, I gave her Gus' number. Manny wouldn't be in until the night shift.

"Detective Ferguson," Gus said when he answered.

"Hey, it's me."

"What's up?"

"I'm over at Mount Sinai. Got a call from the duty doctor earlier. Apparently, there was a strange man in snooping around. I just finished interviewing the duty nurse, a Mrs. Williams. She confronted the guy. Says he said something about looking for a friend. When she asked for the friend's name, he split."

"Hmm. You thinkin' this guy was looking for Gabe?"

"Be my guess," I said.

"You get a description?"

"Yeah. A pretty good one and, no, before you ask, he isn't one of the guys that attacked him."

"So? What're you thinkin'?"

"I'm thinking that it was crony. Someone connected to them somehow. Maybe a convert or another southerner. And something else. I got another call from a contact letting me know that there are a couple guys nosing around looking for information on me. Said they weren't southerners either."

"You do have a way of stirrin' up the shit, don't you."

"Best way to find what you're after sometimes."

"Okay. So you obviously got their attention. Now what?"

"I figure they may be trying to cover up their loose ends, thinking that there may be something that would bring you down on them. Don't forget, they're probably the ones responsible for killing that old black man the other night."

"So you think that if they take you out, it'll stop anymore interest in them for the murder and Gabe's beating? I don't think so. This ain't Mississippi or wherever."

"Hey, like I said before, these guys haven't been showing much in the smarts department, otherwise they wouldn't still be here. But, yeah, that is exactly what I think they're thinking."

"Okay, but why scope out where Gabe is?"

"Obviously, because they think he can finger the guys that did him."

"Hmm. Makes sense. So what're gonna do?"

"Well, for now, I'm going to continuing trying to build a case to hand over to Manny. As for Gabe, I think he's safe enough here for now. These guys don't have the skill or resources to make a run on him here...I hope, but to make sure, I think I'll put someone in here just in case."

"Who ya got in mind?"

"You remember Charlie Russell?"

"Over in that gym you workout at?"

"Yeah. He's a good man and tough enough so it won't be easy to get past him."

"I remember. What about once they cut him loose?" Gus asked.

"I'll cross that bridge if I have to later. I hope that this will be over before then and there'll be nothing to worry about."

"Okay. Keep in touch and watch your ass," Gus said.

"Yes, Dad," I said then hung up.

I made one more call to Maggie.

"Hey, boss. Glad you called. Where are you by the way?"

"Still at the hospital and before you ask, Gabe's doing great. Something come in?" I asked.

"Yeah. Got a call from the Chez Marie's. Someone was in asking about Gabe. You know, stuff like his name and where he lived, that sort of stuff," Maggie said.

"Okay, thanks. Good to know."

"That mean Gabe's in danger?"

"Not anymore. I'm going to put Charlie Russell on the floor to watch over him."

"Thank God for that. He's good."

"Yeah. Anything else?"

"One of my contacts called. I think I got an address for the missing girl. You want me to go check it out?" said.

"Yeah, okay, do that, by the way, you still carrying?"

"Uh-huh."

"Good. Be careful. If it looks bad, don't take any chances, got it?"

"Uh-huh," she said.

"Good. See you tomorrow," I said then hung up.

I left the room and walked down the hall to Gabe's room. I peeked in and saw that he was asleep. He was still bandaged up, but somehow, he did look a lot better. I returned to the nurse's station.

"I peeked in on my friend but he's asleep. Could you let him know I was stopped by," I said.

"Certainly," Mrs. Williams said.

"Oh, and another thing. If it is at all possible, could you let the other nurses know about this guy that was here, you know, a description or something like that," I said.

"If you think that is necessary," she said. "I'll need to clear it with the doctor, but I'm sure it'll be okay. I'll have a description typed up and place on the board there," she said, indication a. corkboard on the wall.

"Do you think he may come back?"

"It's possible, yeah, but don't worry about it. I'm going to have a friend of mine come over and stay with Gabe. He won't be in the way or anything like that, but he'll be near by in case this guy comes back."

"He won't have a gun or anything like that will he? I couldn't agree to that if he does," she said, her voice expressing real concern.

"No, he'll be unarmed. His name is Charlie Russell. Just call him Charlie."

"Charlie Russell, got it. How long will he stay here?"

"Only during your regular visiting hours. However, he'll also stay an extra hour in the canteen downstairs, just in case."

"So, what do I do if this man comes back? Get Charlie?"

"Not unless you need him. He's here to watch Gabe. If this man does come back, call this number right away and speak to either Detective Ferguson or Detective Rodriquez. Tell them you're calling on my advise."

"Okay," she said, taking the piece of paper I used to write down the phone number. "Is this man dangerous? Would he hurt any of my...?"

"No, I don't think so. But, if he shows up again, don't confront him, just make that call. The cops are close by and can be here very quickly."

"Okay," she said, still sounding a bit upset.

"Seriously, you don't need to be afraid. These guys aren't the sort to use force." I hoped.

"Okay," she said, again. "Do you want us to call you too?"

"Not necessary. Just call that number. Thanks again for all your help and for what you're doing for Gabe."

"All in a day's work," she said with a half smile.

I said goodbye and left. Once outside, I headed for the gym where I work out. One of its main functions is as a fight training gym. I had a number of good contacts there that I sometimes worked with when I needed to 'touch up' a little. I knew a couple of the regulars really well and have used them before.

When you first walk into a gym where boxers are training you are struck by the sounds and smells. The first thing you hear is the rhythmic cadence of thumps as men work on the heavy bags mixed in with the sharp rapid staccato of others working on the speed bags and still others skipping, the ropes whistling through the air. All this mingled with the chants from trainers putting their 'boys' through their drills. Then there's the unique odour of sweat mingled with seasoned leather and canvas. Machismo at its best.

I walked inside, saying hello to a few of the men that I knew, as I went looking for Charlie Russell.

He was over in a corner holding a heavy bag for a young black kid who was pounding away on it with some very solid jabs and crosses. I saw Charlie jolt after each hit. I pity the poor bastard that ends up on the wrong end of those punches.

Charlie Russell was once considered a prospect to go all the way to the top about ten years ago. That all ended during a fight when his opponent gave him a severe jab to ribs, breaking two of them and sending one into a lung. The fight game was all he knew so, when he recovered, he signed on with his former manager as a trainer.

Charlie stood about five-eight and was built like the proverbial brick shit house. Fifty-inch-chest. Forty-two-inch waist. Twenty-inch neck, if anyone would call that a neck. Arms like tree trunks. You get the idea. He was a skilled fighter. A 'natural' those in the business called him. I often heard some fighters who went into the ring against him, say the thing they remember most was taking a hit from him was like being hit by a runaway truck. I sparred with him enough to know, even though his punches with me were pulled. I still knew I had been hit.

"Hey, Murph," Charlie said when he spotted me. "Lookin' fer a workout?"

"Not today, Charlie. You got a few minutes we can talk?"

"Yeah, sure, we 'bout done 'ere. Take ten on the speed, Joey, then hit the showers," he said to the kid.

"Okay, Charlie," the kid said, as he walked away, still shadow punching. Christ, he didn't even look like he broke a sweat.

"Looks good," I said as we walked to a bench against the nearby wall.

"Got potential. Might have a shot someday," Charlie said, flipping a towel over his head and onto his shoulders.

"Okay spill," he said when we sat down.

"I got a little job for you. Baby-sitting," I said.

"Okay. When and where?"

"As soon as you can get away. The where is over at Mount Sinai."

"A hospital? Who's da baby?"

"You know Gabe Herschon? Works over at Chez Marie's?"

"Queer dude, right?"

I ignored the slight and nodded.

"Yeah, I 'eard of 'im. Didn't I jus' hear sumthin' 'bout 'im gettin' a beatin'?"

"Yeah. Pretty bad too. Jumped by three guys. Klansmen up from the South."

"Yeah, been hearin' stories 'bout dese guys too. So whaddya need?"

"I think they might try and finish the job to prevent him from talking to the cops."

"Uh-huh. Dey packin' or anythin'?"

I shook my head. "Not that I heard, but that doesn't mean they aren't. I don't need you to take them on, that's my end. What I do need is someone who can deal with anybody who shows up with unfriendly ideas."

"Okay. I'm in. How long?"

"A couple of days, three tops. How's fifty a day sound?"

"Cool. I'll clear it with Jackie and head right over after I hit the showers."

"Great. When you get there, go to the second floor, ask for a nurse named Kathy Williams. She's expecting you. She'll give you a run down on the guy who has already showed up. You stay during regular visiting hours then an extra hour in the canteen, just in case. Keep a low profile."

"Okay. Done. Thanks, Murph. The extra bread'll come in handy," Charlie said.

I pulled out my wallet and fished out two twenties and a ten and passed it to him.

"I told her to call the cops right away if this guy comes back. All you got to do is make sure he doesn't get into Gabe's room."

"No sweat."

Deal done, I decided to head on home.

Chapter Fourteen

Later, after putting the kids to bed and spending a little quality time with my wife, which meant a little sweet love making, then a quick shower, I headed back out.

My plan was to cruise the Park area in the hope of finding a trace of the two men. I also wanted to nose around in some of the bars, cafes, and clubs, and talk to people I knew to see if they could steer me in some sort of direction. It didn't take me long.

I ran into a street hustler I knew. He was known around the area as, Mickey the Mouse, don't ask why, no one knew, but many just called him Mickey Mouse. I never knew his last name. I don't think many did.

He was about fifty or so, if his receding hairline was anything to go by. Standing around five-six and lanky. Overall, he looked pretty nondescript except for his constant moving – couldn't keep still; always looking from side to side, as if he expecting someone to jump out at him at any minute. Sort of reminded you of the stand-up comic, Rodney Dangerfield.

In many ways he was a lot like another 'character' I once knew, Crazy Pete, though not quite so eccentric. Still, Mickey had his finger on the pulse of the goings-on in the Park in the same way Pete used to have his on the Village.

I spotted him outside a club making his pitch to a pair of couples out for the night. Young, maybe late twenties. They had a middle class look about them; you see them 'slumming' around the Park and Village, mostly on weekend nights, looking some of the fun they heard or read about.

"Hey. Ya lookin' for somethin' innerestin'?" I heard him say to them when I came within earshot.

The two women stood slightly behind their dates. Must've thought Mickey might have something contagious on him, I thought, watching this little bit of street theatre unfold.

"No thanks," one of the men said,trying to push past him with a look of disdain.

"Whazza matter, eh? 'Fraid a little excitement? C'mon. Good way to impress da skirts, eh? Maybe git lucky later, whaddya say, huh?"

"What? What did you just say?" the young man demanded in a loud voice. I could see this wasn't going to end well. What the man didn't know was Mickey always carried a shiv up the sleeve of his coat and was good with it.

I moved quickly between them just as Mickey's hand flexed to retrieve the blade.

"Who the hell are you?" the man said, looking a little startled at my sudden appearance.

"The man who's about to save you from something you won't like," I said.

He stood there looking at me, well, maybe more like he glaring at me.

"Wh..what are you...?" he started to say before I cut him off.

"Just walk away. Okay?"

He hesitated trying to decide whether discretion, and all that, was the right move to make.

"I wouldn't advise it, son," I said, evenly and with enough of an edge in my voice to let him know not to go there.

"Come on, Phillip. Let's get away from here," the young brunette standing behind him said, sounding very nervous. "I want to leave."

He hesitated a moment longer then turned on his heel and hurried off, his date clinging tightly to his arm.

"Aw, geez, Murph. Why'd cha hafta do dat for? I woulda only give him a little souvenir," Mickey whined as the couples moved off down the sidewalk.

"Not worth it," I said. "So, how come you're hawking for some rip-off joint?"

"Gotta make a buck, yeah. 'Sides, who sez it's a rip-off joint?"

I gave him an incredulous look.

"Yeah, yeah, okay. I owe's da owner. Anyway, whacha doin' down here dis late? Ain't seen ya out for a long time."

"I'm working on something," I said.

"Figures. Ya come lookin' fer me, yeah?"

"Yeah," I said. Good to score a point by letting him think he had something I needed. "You know anything about some southerners been up around here hassling the gays?"

He nodded.

"What can you tell me?"

"Les' see, mmm, talk better wit a cold beer goin' down."

"Lead the way," I said.

We went inside and took a spot at the end of the bar. He signalled the bartender with two fingers. A moment later, he came over with two bottles of beer.

"Shoot," I said, taking a sip of the beer.

"Well, way I hear it, these assholes been cruisin' da neighbourhood hasslin' da queers an' freaks. Most a the time dey jus' run dere mouths an' do a bit a shovin'. Nuttin' serious, ya know, jus' anuff to scare the little shits."

"You make it sound like there're a lot of these guys running around," I said.

"Naw. I hear there's no more 'n a half dozen maybe."

"You know any of these guys? Where they hang out or live?"

"Hmm, yeah, maybe. there's this one guy, Dixon, Jimmy Dixon that's it. Shows up 'bout a year or so back. Real hardass."

"No one else?"

"I see sum other guys with him once. Rough trade. Cuppla punks. Don't think they from down home; didn't speak with that stupid accent. So, what's yer interest in these guys?"

"I'm only interested in getting my hands on two guys in particular," I said.

"I'm guessin' it ain't these two then?"

"Right. However, I might be interested in them. Look. You interested in making a few bucks?"

"Is the Pope Catholic?"

"I need a couple of things. First, the whereabouts of the two guys I want." I gave him a description of them. "And let me know if you hear anyone askin' around about me or Gabe."

"Yeah, sure, I kin do dat. What's in it fer me?"

"Twenty," I said.

"Up front?" he asked, pushing his hand, palm up, toward me.

I took out a twenty-dollar bill and placed it in his hand.

"Another one when you get what I want."

He stuffed the bill into his shirt pocket then said, "How soon you need it?"

"As quick as you can manage it," I said. "If you get something, call my office and leave a message."

"Gotcha. That it?"

"Yeah, for now," I said. "Want another one?"

"Naw, I'm good."

"Okay. I'm going to hang around the area for a few hours. Check out some of the other places. I'll pass by later and see if you got anything."

"Work's fer me," he said, getting up and finishing his beer. He put the glass on the table then headed for the street.

I checked my watch: ten-thirty, time for another beer and take a few minutes to consider my next step.

Queen's Park has two faces: by day it is one of the city's popular parks with its walkways and green spaces where people come to sit and relax. Then at night it morphs into a popular cruising area for members of the gay community, mostly men; for some reason gay women steer clear of the area. Then, there is the real dark side of the night scene: the hustlers, pimps, pushers and punks. It is the peculiar nature of these two opposite worlds – the safe and the dangerous - that make it such a fascinating place.

I walked around the neighbourhood for a few hours, stopping to talk with some of my old contacts I spotted along the way. I got a lot of 'Hey Murphs, long time no see' but not much else. A few of my older contacts were no longer around and some of the newer people didn't know me, though some had heard about me.

The streets that circled the Park were busy as usual with lookers, young people hanging around a few coffee shacks who couldn't afford to go in. I had hoped that Mickey might have picked something up, but I hadn't seen him.

By twelve-thirty and after a few beers, I was getting tired and gaining no more information than I already had, so I decided to call it a night and went back to see Mickey. He said he couldn't find out anything more than he already told me. He said that he might have better luck in a day or two. I told him not to bother, but if he did pick up anything to call me. I fished out another ten spot and gave it to him then headed for my car and home.

* * *

Jake and Bobby Lee were hanging out in their car with Cletus when Bobby Lee suddenly spotted Murphy.

"I'll be Gawdamned," he said, tapping Jake on his arm. "Lookee there."

"What?" Jake said, looking over his shoulder.

"It's him. That PI, Murphy."

"Huh? Where?"

"There, yonder, jus' passin' that drugstore," Bobby Lee said, pointing. "The guy in da hat."

They both watched as Murphy navigated through the crowded sidewalk.

"You sure?" Jake asked.

"Yep. It's him. Whadda we do?"

"Let's go. Follow him, see where he's goin'. Maybe we kin git a chance an' take him."

"Okay."

"Listen, we'll catch y'all up later, Clete. We got sum business to take care of, okay?"

"Yeah, sure, man. No sweat. Y'all need some hep?" Cletus asked.

"Naw. This ain't yer affair. Thanks."

"Okay. Later."

They quickly crossed over to other side of the street, dodging the cars and cabs causing them to lay on their horns. Murphy was almost a full block ahead of them by now. They pushed their way through the people catching a few choice words for the effort. Jake saw him turn at the corner.

"C'mom," he said as he quickened his step. "We're gonna lose him."

They reached the corner just in time to see him cross over to the other side which, for some reason, was less crowded.

"Whadda we do now?" Bobby Lee asked as they stopped and watched him.

"I'm thinkin'," Jake said.

"Damn. Whaddya figure he was doin' over here this late?"

"Dunno, lookin' fer us be my guess."

"Jee-sus. How'd he figure out we was here so quick?"

"Dunno but I'm thinkin', Maxie."

"Ya think?"

"Makes most sense as anythin' I kin think of," Jake said.

"Where ya think he's headin'?" Bobby Lee asked.

"His car, maybe, I dunno know."

"So, what? We stay on him?"

"Naw. Too risky. 'Sides, nuttin' we kin do 'round here anyway."

Jake turned around and headed back down the street with Bobby Lee close behind him.

"Too bad," Bobby Lee said. Wudda been nice to take him out."

"Yeah," Jake said. "Let's head over an' see Jimmy."

* * *

I was walking back to my car when I heard several cars laying on their horns. I glance over my shoulder just in time to spot the man that tried tailing me a couple of days ago with another man playing dodge cars in the middle of a busy street.

He must've made me, I thought, and were following me hoping to get their chance at me. Okay, I said softly to myself. "Let's do it."

I knew of a vacant lot not far from where I parked my car. I would lead them there and bushwhack them.

When I reached the corner, I turned left and when I was about a third of the way up the street, cut out of the crowd and crossed over to other side. I took a quick look back to make sure they were still behind me. They were but had stopped at the corner.

Damn it, I thought, they weren't coming after me. I couldn't let them know that I made them, so I couldn't double back after them because I'd lose the edge. Well, at least, I knew for certain that they were now over here in the Park. I continued heading for my car.

* * *

When I went downstairs to the office in the morning, Maggie was at her desk as usual shuffling through papers. She looked up and smiled, it is one of the nice things I look forward to each morning. Today she was wearing a pale pink angora short sleeve sweater that stretched just enough to accent her perky breasts perfectly. I knew she had a snug fitting skirt on as well, she always wore a skirt, or a dress. She has great looking legs and knew it. Better enjoy it as long as I can. I knew it wouldn't be long before her belly would begin to grow.

She passed me a folded newspaper and said the coffee was freshly made. I poured a mug of coffee and headed for my office.

I put the paper and mug down on the desk and picked up the phone. I wanted to call Manny before he left. Unfortunately, he wasn't in, so I spoke with Gus Ferguson instead.

"What's up?" he said, when he came on line.

"I was hoping to get Manny but missed him," I said.

"Yeah. He caught a bug or something. Didn't make it in last night. So. Whaddya got?"

"Right. I was over in the Park last night. You know, dropping in on some of the old places, talking with some of my old contacts. Anyway, remember when I told you about picking up that tail the other day?"

"Uh-huh."

"Well, guess who I spotted late last night?"

"Same fella."

"You got it. Though this time he wasn't alone. I think the other man is the second one I'm looking for," I said.

"So, that means you were right, guessing that these guys are now over here. Now what? You still got nothin' we can use to take them in."

"I know. I got someone looking into it as we speak. By the way, my guy passed on the name of someone these guys might be hooked up with, maybe even helping them. Says he's another southerner. Jimmy Dixon. Suppose to have digs somewhere on Manning. Don't suppose you'd have a sheet on him?"

"I'll leave a message for Manny to check it out. He's got a contact works that area,"

Gus said. "This guy you're using, he's reliable?"

"Remember Crazy Pete?"

"Yeah. 'Nough said. You plannin' on payin' a visit to this Dixon?"

"Thought I might," I said.

"You know that if he's connected to these guys you could be walkin' into a situation, right?"

"Chance I gotta take. I want to get this business done."

"Okay, jus' watch your ass. By the way, you manage to get Charlie on the job?"

"Yeah. He started last night."

"Okay. I'll fill Manny in when he comes in or, if he's out for aa few days, I'll look into it."

"Thanks. Later," I said then hung up.

I picked up the paper and scanned the front paper. The main headers were about the big issues of the day: Vietnam, Russia, Cuba and so on. I quickly flipped through the first section then took a peek at the sports page. I'm not what you call a sports fan but every once in a while I like to see how the local big name teams were doing. I finally went to the section with items on the various boroughs, including the Village.

There were all the usual items: who was in town, playing around the club circuit, short cryptic paragraphs about the bad shit that happened and police reports but, happily, no beatings or attacks on gays or anyone else.

A half hour later, Maggie came in carrying a fresh mug of coffee and sat in one of the client chairs in front of the desk.

"Thanks," I said, when she set the mug down. I folded the paper and set it aside on the desk.

"So? Anything new?" she asked. This was also part of our morning routine.

"Not much. I now know these guys are in the Park area now, and may have a lead to them. His name is Jimmy Dixon. Lives somewhere near by. I also hooked up with Mickey."

"The Mouse?" she asked.

"Uh-huh. Nobody knows more about what's happenin' in the Park area. He's the one gave me this Dixon guy. He'll be calling in at times, so just take the information, okay?"

"Okay. So, you going to look into the Dixon fella?"

"Uh-huh," I said, glancing at my watch, "I'm heading back over there in about an hour. I'll call in regularly."

"Okay."

"By the way, how's it going on the Harding case?"

"I think I got a lead on where the girl is staying. It's over on Huron Street. Sounds like a hippie flop. I'm waiting on one more call to confirm it. If she's there, what do you want me to do?"

Huron Street was one of several east of Yorkville where the transient hippies gravitated to and subsequently settled in a one of many houses as crashers or squatters. Overall, these areas were relatively quiet and safe, so far. The only real danger came from pushers; sometimes the odd dealer. If the girl was holed up there then something else could be behind her running away.

I took a moment to consider her question, then said, "If you're up to it, can you make contact with her? See if she'll talk to you, you know, woman to woman. Might actually be better than being confronted by a man."

"Yeah, I can do that," Maggie said. "Good thinking. Might be that it was because of a man she took off."

"You'd think that, right!" I said, pretending to be offended.

"Oh you. You know what I mean," Maggie shot back with a smile. She knew I was kidding.

"Yeah. Just keep good notes for the report."

"Right," she said, standing up and smoothing down her skirt which had slid up several inches exposing two very nice-looking thighs. I smiled.

"Behave yourself or I'll tell Jane," she said as she turned and headed back to her desk.

"I'll try," I said, trying to sound like a lecherous old man. We didn't have that kind of banter too often but when we do, it is always innocent and playful.

It was nearing noon when I finally decided to head out for my return trip to the Park. I still hadn't heard from Mickey which wan't surprising. Like so many of what I call, 'the night crawlers of the Village', he didn't often get up during the daytime.

I almost made it out the door when the phone rang. It was Gus. I took the call at Maggie's desk.

"What's up?" I said into the mouthpiece.

"Just got off the phone with a friend of mine over in PR. Sez he's heard of this Dixon fella you mentioned," Gus said.

PR is a new public relations initiative set up by the Mayor to improve community relations. In actuality, it was an intelligence gathering unit set up to get information on the so-called radicals that seemed to be popping up all over the city: the anti-war protesters, the gay movement activists, the politically active black movement up from the States.

"Yeah, and...?"

"Seems this guy is known to be a shit disturber, running 'round the pushing a lotta crap against the Papists, Jews, gays, and blacks. You get the picture, pretty much anybody don't think like them. Anyway, seems he's been under surveillance for a while."

"Any arrests?"

"Nope. He doesn't do his own dirty work, but my guy thinks he's definitely behind several attacks."

"Interesting. Your friend say anything else?"

"Yeah, he's been seen with three others on a regular basis. From what he said, two of them sound like the ones you're after. I got a feeling the third guy was the one fished out of the lake the other day."

"Uh-huh. Did he say if this Dixon is known to be violent?"

"Didn't say. My guess is no. He gets others to do the dirty work. Anyway, he had an address on him."

"That's okay. Already got it. Thanks Gus, appreciate this," I said.

"No sweat. Oh, yeah, one more thing. Seems Gabe thinks he can ID one of the guys attacked him. I sending someone over to talk to him and get a description."

"Okay, thanks. I think I'll stop by and have a quick chat myself. By the way, how's Manny feeling?"

"Better. Sez he'll be in tonight."

"Good to hear. I'll touch base with him later. Bye." I hung up the phone.

"Everything okay?" Maggie asked, looking up at me.

"Yeah. Gus had some follow up information for me. I'm going over and check in on Gabe, then I'll be over in the Park area for the rest of the day. I call in."

"Okay," she said. "Say hi for me."

"Will do."

When I arrived at the hospital, I spotted Charlie Russell sitting on a chair across from Gabe's room, reading a paper. It looked like the nurses must have found him one of these portable table things that you see over a patient's bed. It was beside him and had a pitcher of water, a glass, and a food tray on it.

"Looks like the nurses are treating you well," I said, as I approached him.

"Yeah. They're really nice people, ya know, an' none too hard on the eyes either," he said, folding the paper and setting it on the table.

"Nothing shaking, I take it?"

"Nope. Jus' a few visitors is all."

"Visitors?"

"Yeah, ya know, his people," Charlie said.

"Oh, right, gotcha," I said. His people meant, gays.

"Ya gonna be here for a few minutes," he asked, standing up.

I nodded.

"Great. I gotta hit da can." He turned and headed off down the hall.

I opened the door to Gabe's room and stepped inside.

"Hi, Gabe," I said.

He was sitting up and looked a lot better. He broke into a broad smile when he saw me.

"Murph," he said, breaking into a smile.

"Looks like you're feeling a lot better," I said, pulling one of the visitors chairs next to the bed and sitting down.

"Yes, I am. Wonderful people here. They treat me so well."

"That's good to hear."

"I suppose you're here to talk some more about what happened, yes?"

"Some, yeah. But I also want to make sure you're doing okay," I said.

"I know. And I truly appreciate it. So. What do you want to talk about?"

"I got a call from Gus Ferguson this morning, you remember him," Gabe nodded, "well, he told me you remember one of the men that attacked you."

"That's right."

"And you're going to give the police a description of the guy?"

He nodded, "Yes."

"Good for you. That takes guts."

"I'm not afraid of these people, Murph. They are ignorant cowards. I saw worse before I came to this country."

"That's what I figured," I said. "Can you give me that description?"

"Certainly, but why? The police are going to handle this, aren't they?"

"Yeah, they will, but you been around long enough to know they can only put so much time on this, whereas I can deal with it exclusively."

"But you don't need to," Gabe said.

I raised an eyebrow and looked at him. He just smiled.

"Okay. So tell me," I said.

He said he could only remember one of the men that attacked him. The one that did the beating. He remember that there were three of them. One stayed outside the alley while the other two pulled in. One held him while the other hit him. He gave me a good description of this one. It matched the information I already had on these guys.

"That's great, Gabe, thanks. It matches up with what I've already picked up," I said when he finished.

"Do you think you'll be able to find these men?"

I nodded. "Yeah, I'm pretty sure I can get them."

"Then what?"

"I'll hand them over to the cops with enough evidence to bust them. Your description, and what I have, should be enough to bring charges for aggravated assault against at least two of them. They should end up doing some time, or at least, turn them over to the U.S. authorities. Don't forget, they're deserters."

"Amen to that," Gabe said.

"Right," I said, standing up. "So, you need anything before I go?'

"No, no, I'm good, thanks. And thanks for Charlie out there. I guess you think they might come back?"

I shrugged. 'You know me. I like to be cautious."

"Well, it's much appreciated."

"Okay. Get your rest and we'll talk again soon."

Back in the hall, I saw that Charlie was back and sitting at his post.

"Okay, I'm off," I said.

"Okay, see ya," he said, picking up his paper again.

I checked the nurse's station as I walked by looking for Mrs. Williams but she wasn't there, probably wasn't on duty, or was somewhere on the ward. I headed for the parking lot and back to the office.

When I got there Maggie wasn't at her usual place. I spotted the note taped to my door.

'Made contact with the girl. Have gone to meet with her.

Be back soon. M.'

Good news, I thought, as I poured a coffee and went into my office.

Maggie returned around two-thirty. After taking off her coat, she came into the office and sat down. She had a wide grin on her face.

"Everything went well, I take it?" I said, waiting for her to report.

"Better. We had a long talk and she filled me in on everything."

"So, is she willing to see her mother?"

"Maybe. Depends on how she responds to what we tell her about why Caroline left,"

"Go ahead. Tell me," I said.

"Right. Seems the main reason she left was because of another girl. This one is a couple of years older, and gay. Seems that Caroline is very introverted and shy and took to this other girl who, I'm guessing, seduced her. Anyway, according to Caroline, everything that happened between them was voluntary on her part."

"Okay, so why come here?" I asked.

"You know what Scarborough is like. Family wouldn't handle the possible scandal. What they were doing wasn't looked upon as acceptable. Too many problems for them and, especially her family. So they decided to leave and come here. They heard about the large community of gays in the Village and thought they'd have less problems being with like minded people."

"Yeah, makes sense. The gays been around here a long time. Don't know about being a safer or more accepting place though," I said. "What about this other girl? The one she ran off with, you see her?"

"Uh-huh," Maggie said, nodding. "Her name is Casey Fillmore. Age: twenty. Known each other a couple of years they say. Live in the same neighbourhood. Both girls are pretty average looking, not real head turners, you know what I mean. Guess they got left out of a lot of stuff at school. Not a lot of boys probably paid them much attention. Easy to see why they gravitated to each other."

"Funny how every place has kids like that," I said when she paused. "But things often change as they get a bit older."

"I know, but she has to learn that for herself, I suppose. So do we call the mother, have her come in and then lay all this on her?" Maggie asked.

I nodded. "Uh-huh. It's what she paid us to do," I answered.

Maggie sat looking at me for several seconds before speaking again. She read the look on my face.

"Let me guess. You want me to be the one to break the news to her that her daughter is living in the Village as a lesbian?"

"Makes sense, don't you agree," I said. "Besides, I think she would be embarrassed, maybe even ashamed, hearing it come from a man."

"Yeah, I understand that but it's just that..."

"I know, baby. That's one of the downsides of the job; telling clients things they won't want to hear."

"Okay. I'll call her and ask her to come in," Maggie said, standing up. "I'll write up my report and make a copy for her. You got any more billing to charge her?"

"No. That last payment about covered everything," I said.

"Okay."

"That's my girl," I said. "By the way, if it helps, you did a first-rate job on this, your first solo case."

That put a smile on her face as she headed to her desk.

Chapter Fifteen

Three men sat around a chrome table in the small kitchen idly chatting. There was an open bottle of whisky sitting on the table next to a half full ashtray.

Jake was in the living room talking with someone on the phone. The conversation was mostly one sided with Jake doing the listening.

"Uh-huh. Got it. You're sure 'bout this?" he said.

"Yeah. Word just came in at the desk for Silvano from someone a half hour ago," the voice on the other end of the line said.

"Okay," Pickett said. "We'll take care of it."

"By the way, I don't think I'm gonna be able to help you guys anymore. I think they might be onto me."

"How do ya know?"

"Call it a hunch. So I'm gonna lay low for a while. Good luck."

"Okay. Thanks. Y'all git back in touch when ya can, hear."

"Okay," he said then hung up.

Jake hung up the phone and went back to the others.

"Whazzup?" Jimmy Dixon asked when Jake sat down.

"That was Dillon, my cop contact Maxie set me up with. He sez that he's heard soumthin' 'bout that fag we did a few nights back. Seems he remembers one of us an' is gonna give a description to the cops."

"Shit," Bobby Lee said. "Shudda killed him."

"Yeah, maybe, but y'all didn't, an' now we got us another problem ta deal with," Dixon said.

"Ya mean beside da peeper?" the fourth man asked.

Dixon looked at him and nodded.

"Ya want me an' summa da boys ta take care a him?"

Dixon thought about this for several moments before speaking.

"Y'all think ya kin do it an' git away wit it?" he asked.

"Piece a cake," the man said. "Jus' say da word."

"It'd be risky," Jake said, "'specially iff'n the cops are onto us."

"I know, but this guy is turnin' inta a real pain in da ass," Bobby Lee said.

"Yeah, I know. But I ain't so sure we could do him without drawing a lot of heat and not jus' from da cops. Don't fergit, he's friendly wit summa them niggers that's lookin' fer us too," Jake added.

"Man, sure wish we was back home. We could really show this prick sumthin'," Bobby Lee said.

"Yeah, well, this ain't home," Jake snapped.

"Cut it out you two," Dixon said. "We gotta figure this out afore y'all find yer asses in jail."

"Yeah, okay," Jake said, reaching for the whisky.

"Alright," Bobby Lee said, pushing his glass across the table toward Jake.

"So, do we take care of Murphy or the queer?" Dixon asked.

"Why not both?" Jake said, pouring a shot of booze into the two glasses.

"Mmm, makes sense, I s'pose," Dixon said, leaning forward. "How'd we go at?"

"Me an' a coupla guys kin take care a Murphy, an' Bobby Lee with one his guys could do the queer."

"Hmm, maybe," Dixon responded. "But I'm thinkin' you an' Bobby Lee take care a the faggot, an' Kelly here kin get summa his boys an' take care a Murphy."

"Makes sense, We know Murphy probably would recognize us before we could do anything," Jake said. Kelly an' me kin git inta the hospital easy enough, 'specially iff'n the cops are hangin' around the place."

"Ya sure y'all kin git inside an' do what need's doin'?"

"No sweat," Jake said.

"How y'all figure to do him?"

"Easy. Smother the fucker with his own pillow. Quick an' quiet. No noise. No fuss. In an' out. Easy."

"Okay, but what about the nurses?"

"No problem. We go in right after lunch when the place is busy."

"An' how y'all plan to take out Murphy?" Dixon asked, looking at Kelly. "This guy ain't no pushover."

"Take 'im at his office. Use a silencer. Jus' go in an' pow." Kelly said, pointing his finger like a pistol.

"Yeah, that could work. How quick kin you organize your guys?" Dixon asked Kelly.

"Quick. I'll make some calls now," he said, standing up and heading for the phone.

"Okay. Git yer guys to meet up here, then Jake and Bobby Lee, you head for the hospital. Kelly, you head for Murphy's office. Jake's got da address. Y'all need any hardware?"

"Nah, we're good. I know just the guys for dis," Kelly said as he started to dial. "Good guys."

"Make sure they're heeled," Jake put in. "By the way, when it's done you an' the boys'll have to split; get outta the city, maybe head for Montreal, or back over the border for a spell."

"No sweat."

"Right. That's settled then. I gotta take off. Y'all know da plan so, Jake, you take care that it goes off like we jus' talked," Dixon said, standing up.

"Okay," Jake said. "We'll call ya when it's done."

"Good huntin'," Dixon said as he headed out of the apartment leaving the three men behind.

* * *

On the drive to the address I had on Dixon, I had time to work a out a plan. I had one major problem to overcome: I didn't have a solid description for him, which meant I would have to ask around. Risky at best. I didn't know any of the people I'd have to speak to, any of whom could warn him that I was looking for him, and if I did manage to find him, it was possible I wouldn't catch him alone. But if I did, then what? Reasoning with him didn't seem like an option given their recent activities. Threatening him? Maybe. But with what? Oh well, I thought, guess I'd just have to trust to my famous luck and deal with whatever presents itself at the time.

I suddenly thought that I heard a familiar soft sound of chuckling in the back of my mind...

When I arrived at the street where he supposedly lived, I found an empty slot about a third of the way down the street and steered my car alongside the curb. I pulled my gun out and eased the safety off and re-holstered it. I got out and locked the door, took a quick look at the street numbers and

224

saw that my destination was about two buildings to my right.

Traffic on the street was moderately busy and the sidewalks were crowded with pedestrians, a lot looked like students, not surprising considering how close I was to the University of Toronto campus.

I crossed over to opposite side of the street from where Dixon lived. This would give me a better angle of view as I neared his place. I scanned the surrounding area looking for the Chevy my guys used just in case they were here. Nothing.

Everything looked normal so I headed over to the building where he lived. I climbed the steps and entered the small foyer. There was a panel with one row of yellowed buttons on the wall showing that were nine units in the building. All but two had names printed on paper tags beside them. Dixon was one of the missing ones. The first blank was for an apartment on the first floor, number two, the second was on the top floor, number seven.

I buzzed one of the apartments on the same floor as the blank tag. If someone answered, I would ask if this was Dixon. If I got lucky, perhaps they would tell me which apartment was his.

There was no response from the one on the first floor. I tried the next one.

"Yes?" a woman said, her voice sounding tinny through the intercom.

"Is Jimmy there?" I said, leaning close to the panel.

"Who?"

"Jimmy Dixon. Is he there?"

"No, there's no Jimmy here," she said. "I think he lives on the top floor."

"Oh, sorry, my mistake," I said.

"That's okay," she said. Then I heard the click as she broke the connection.

Just at that moment, I spotted someone, a young woman through the glass panel in the door. I pulled out my keyring and made like I was about to unlock the door just as she was arrived. I stepped aside as she opened it and walked past me, giving her a smile as she went by. I slipped in behind her.

I headed up to the top floor. The building was old but fairly well maintained and clean. There was the occasional cry of a baby from one of the units but otherwise it was quiet. I figured most of the residents were probably at their jobs or out. I arrived on the top floor and walked to apartment number seven.

I stopped at the door and listened for anything inside. All I heard was the sound of music from a radio. I listened a moment longer, then heard the muffled sound of men talking but couldn't make out how many.

Now what, I thought, leaning my back against the wall. I decided on my usual approach – direct and hard. I pulled out my gun. If I got lucky, my guys would be inside and that would be an end of this business.

Facing the door, I knocked three times and stepped back, gun levelled.

The door opened a moment later. I tall gaunt looking man stood there staring at me then the gun. He looked about fifty or so with thinning hair and a face that looked like it had gone through everyone of those years.

"Wha...?" he started to say.

"Inside," I said, moving slowly toward him as he started to back away.

Once inside, I closed the door with my foot. There was another man sitting at a wooden kitchen table, a cigarette hanging from his mouth. He didn't look like one of the guys I wanted. There was a bottle of bourbon and a couple of glasses sitting on the table.

"Back to the table and sit down," I said, quickly taking in the rooms.

"Who the fuck are you?"

"Which one of you guys in Dixon?" I asked, staying at least six feet away from the table.

The man sitting at the table shot a quick involuntary glance at the older man.

"I'm looking for a couple of your friends," I said, ignoring his question.

"You're that PI, Murphy. Right?" Dixon said, anger in his voice.

"Right," I said, "and the statement still stands. Where are they?"

"Man, y'all got a set of balls ta come in here wavin' that cannon around. Whaddya goin' ta do, shoot me?"

"I don't have to shoot you. I just need to make a few calls and you either have a shitload of police attention you don't want, or you end up in the morgue. Depending on which phone number I dial."

He gave me a hard look for a brief moment which then changed as he realized the bind he was in.

"So that was you that did KC? He was my cousin," he said, like that would matter somehow in the present situation. I just looked at him, letting him chew on his thoughts.

"What'd we do to piss you off, huh?

"I don't give a shit about the garbage you're trying to sell but I do care about some ignorant assholes damn near beating a friend of mine almost to death. So, again, where are they?"

"Fuck you, faggot lover," he spat.

"Okay. I guess you want to do this the hard way. Fine by me. You'll be done here before the week's over and your buddies'll be in lock up or turned over to the FBI, either way I don't give a shit," I said with a hardness in my tone that he couldn't mistake.

We stared at each other for several moments. I could see the anger and hate in his eyes, but I also saw that he was thinking.

"Here's something else to think on. Even as we're talking, the police are getting a pretty good description from my friend of one of his attackers. So, now you also got to worry about the cops looking for them. Oh, yeah, I almost forgot, there's a coupla really pissed off black dudes I know who're looking for the guys that killed that old man the other night. So ya gotta ask yourself – are they worth the grief that's inching up to your doorstep?"

Jimmy Dixon had a hard choice to make, and he had to make it in front of a witness. I stood there watching him squirm as he struggled with how he was going to get out of this.

"Hey, man, ya gotta do it. The movement is more important than them two boys," the other man said, looking from me to Dixon.

"Fuck," Dixon spat.

"So what's it to be? Talk to me, or do I make some calls?" I said.

"Fuck," he said, again. "Fuck."

"They're gonna take out the faggot before he kin spill to the cops," the man said.

"Jesus, Clete," Dixon snapped.

"Hey, fuck this shit, man. I ain't gittin' wasted 'cause a them boys. Ain't what I signed on for," Cletus said, sounding nervous and scared. "An' I definitely ain't goin' back to the States. The Feds got paper out on me.

"When?" I demanded.

"I dunno. Soon."

"You. When?" I snapped at Dixon.

"Ya heard the man, soon."

"Where are they now?"

"Dunno."

"How many are there?"

No one spoke.

"How many?"

"Jus' Jake an' Bobby Lee," Cletus said.

The two men sat there looking over at me, waiting for my next move. I could see the anger in Dixon while Cletus looked scared. The only one I was worried about doing anything stupid was Dixon.

Keeping an eye on him, I thought over what they just said, trying to put together some sort of plan of action. After a few moments, I made a decision.

"Right. Here's the deal. I leave you two alone, stay outta your business. But, if I hear that you've contacted these guys and warned them that I'm coming, then all bets are off, and you won't be able to move fast enough to avoid the shit storm I'll let loose on your miserable asses. Do you understand?"

"Yeah," Cletus said, nervously.

"You?" I asked, looking at Dixon.

He glared at me with a look that could have fried me right at that moment.

"Well?"

"Yeah," he said through clenched teeth.

"Good. Just a piece of advise, you maybe might want to consider packing up your sick fucking show and head back under the rocks you crawled out from, because the line of horseshit you're peddling just won't fly here," I said.

"Fuck you," Dixon spat, clenching his fists so hard that his knuckles turned white.

I backed my way to the door, my gun still levelled at them. Once in the hall, I beat a hasty retreat back to the street. I had to get over to the hospital as fast as I could.

I had no way of knowing if they were there already or not. The only hope I had was that Charlie could handle the situation if they did show up, and the nurses could call the cops.

Chapter Sixteen

What happened next would prove to be the most dangerous day I lived through since hanging out my shingle.

The three men stopped at the closed door with the name, Matt Murphy stencilled on the glass panel. One of the men pulled out a silenced .38 and reached for the doorknob. The other two moved behind him.

Maggie was sitting at her desk when a silhouette on the glass panel of someone on the other side of the door caught her eye. It didn't move for several moments which, for no particular reason, set off an alarm in her head. She automatically opened the desk drawer where she kept her .22 calibre handgun and wrapped her fingers around it just as the door opened.

The first thing she saw was the silenced gun held waist high. Acting on reflex, she pulled the .22 and squeezed the trigger. The first shot went just wide of the target and embedded in the opposite wall. The second one, however, found its mark, striking the man in his shoulder. Despite being a small calibre gun, the impact jolted him into one of the men closest behind him before falling to the floor.

"Drop it," she yelled, "or I'll put the next one in your head."

The man dropped the gun.

"If there are any others out there with guns, toss them in here." Nothing happened.

"Okay. Whoever is out there get inside and sit down on the floor," she ordered, crouched behind her desk with the gun held in both hands and outstretched across the desktop.

"Okay, sister, take it easy, we ain't armed," a man said as he stepped over his moaning friend lying on the floor clutching his shoulder. A third man followed close behind him.

"Sit," Maggie said through clenched teeth. "Hands in your pockets."

Once all three were on the floor, Maggie slowly stood up keeping the gun on the men. She reached for the phone and dialled.

"Detective Ferguson," Gus said when he answered.

"Gus, it's me, Maggie," she said with a slight tremble in her voice.

"You okay?" Gus asked, sensing that something was wrong.

"Uh-huh. I got three men here. One come in with a gun. I shot one of them."

"Okay. I'm sending someone right over. Can you handle everything til they get there?"

"Yeah. I got them covered," she said, hoping that she sounded confident.

"Right. Ten minutes," Gus said.

"Hurry," Maggie whispered into the mouthpiece then hung up.

She backed away from her desk toward the door to Matt's office and pressed her back against the wall next to it, widening the distance between her and the men, keeping the small pistol held level and steady in her hand.

* * *

Meanwhile, I made it to the hospital in pretty good time. As I drove by, looking for a place to park, I spotted the rebel flag hanging from the aerial of the Chevy. It was parked a block away in front of a florist's shop. I drove past the car and, turning right at the corner, pulled over to the curb. Reaching inside my jacket, I flipped the small leather strap off the hammer of my .38, making sure I could pull it out easily.

The street was busy with pedestrians going about their business. I checked the in the rearview mirror one more time looking for any sign of the black car that had been following me. Nothing. Then I spotted the black car a couple of blocks up the street. It wasn't moving very fast. I guessed they were cruising trying to spot my car. I knew I had to get there ahead of the cops , otherwise when the cops arrived, they would find two dead men; maybe more if anyone else got caught in the crossfire.

I knew I didn't have a lot of time if I really wanted to save Gabe from them. I would have to move fast. I took off for the entrance to the hospital, hoping they wouldn't try and take them inside.

The main lobby area was busy with medical staffers and visitors moving in and out of the facility. I stopped at the main reception desk.

"My name is Matt Murphy. I need you to call this number and tell the cop who answers to get over here as fast as possible," I said, giving her Gus' number.

"Wh...what?   The police...why...what's...?" she stammered.

"Look, just trust me and make the call," I said as I headed for the stairs.

Gabe's room was on the second floor, so I decided to take the stairs instead of the elevator. This might give me the edge if they were already there, since they wouldn't be alerted by the elevator doors opening. Besides, I didn't want to be trapped inside the elevator car if it came to gunplay. As I headed upstairs, I heard shouting and a woman scream. I pulled my gun and took the remaining stairs two at a time stopping at the top to carefully peek around the corner.

Sometimes it's a pain in the ass being me. I had no love for these two men, especially after what they did to Gabe, but I couldn't stand by and let a murder take place if I could prevent it. Like Jane always says: 'I got to be the guy in the white hat'.

No time for subtly. I cocked the hammer and, crouching down, hugged the wall as I neared the top step.

Looking around the corner again, I saw Charlie was struggling to hold off one of the men who was throwing punches at him and slowly pressing him back against the wall. The second man had a pistol in his hand holding it out in front of him as he tried to manoeuvre past them to the door leading into Gabe's room. A nurse, on her hands and knees was crawling back toward the nurse's station. She looked scared but otherwise unhurt. She glanced in my direction. I nodded and waved her to keep heading to the station.

"Hold it right there," I yelled from my position, holding my pistol levelled at the man with the gun.

The one with the gun stopped and started to turn. I recognized him as the one who tried to tail me.

"Don't even think about it," I said, aiming the .38 at his chest. It isn't a good feeling to look down the muzzle of a gun at this range. It inspires second thought...I hoped.

"You!" he spat when he saw me and my gun pointing at him. The other one hesitated when he heard me yell, just long enough for

Charlie to clip him with a solid punch on the jaw, sending him to his knees.

"Drop the gun," I said evenly.

I saw the look come into his eyes. I'd seen it before. It was a mixture of hate and finality. He squeezed the trigger and fired.

I squeezed the trigger twice. The gun jolted sharply in my hand and the corridor filled with the deafening explosions. Everything seemed to suddenly look like it was in slow motion. I watched as the shooter slowly lifted off his feet, his arms falling down, his gun hanging on his curled finger before it dropped to the floor. An instant. That's all it took, then it was over, and everything returned to normal.

"Oh shit," the man at Charlie's feet, muttered, as he watched the dead man crash to the floor, blood spilling out of his body, staining his shirt and pooling on the floor beside him.

"Stupid sonnofabitch," I said, stepping forward. "Why don't they ever listen."

"You shot him, for Chrissake," he said as Charlie grabbed him in a bear hug, pinning his arms to his side.

"You okay, Charlie?" I asked, picking up the dead man's gun by the end of the barrel and putting it in my jacket pocket.

"Yeah, no sweat," Charlie said. It was then that noticed he had a split lip with blood running down his chin, dripping onto his shirt.

"You got him?"

"Yeah."

"Hey, man, why'd cha hafta shoot him?"

"His choice, he shot at me first. Didn't have to go this way. For some stupid reason, I came here to stop you guys and maybe save your sorry asses," I said, easing my way toward the nurse's station.

"What y'all talkin' 'bout, boy? Save our asses?"

"There are some very pissed off black men looking for you two. In fact, they're down in the street right now trying to find me. Now, if it was up to me, I'd be happy to let the brothers have their, uh, 'talk' with you, but fortunately for you, I sort of believe in the rule of law. So, I'm going turn you over to the police and let the courts deal with you."

"'An how y'all figurin' on doin' that?"

"I'm guessing you're the one called, Jake, right?" I said.

"Yeah, so?"

"Nothing. To answer your question, The police are already on the way. So we'll just sit here and wait."

"Y'all fuckin' with the wrong people, ya prick," he said, but without much conviction. He knew he was finished.

"Right," I said, looking down at his dead friend.

After checking on the nurse, Charlie and I put the man in the room where I had interviewed the head nurse a few days ago. Charlie said he could handle him, so I went and looked in on Gabe and, after convincing him everything was okay and this business was over, I went back to the nurse's station to wait for the cops.

Three hours later, I finished up my report and interviews with the police back at the station. Jake Pickett was officially charge with numerous assault charges, second degree murder, and attempted murder based on the evidence I provided.

"Thanks, Murph," Manny said when it was over. "I'll call Silvano and fill him in so he can close his file. You know you were real lucky, right? It could've ended up a whole lot worse."

"Yeah, I know," I said. "Do me a favour and see that I get my gun back, okay?"

He nodded, saying, "Yeah, okay, soon as they're finished with their interviews. Shouldn't be a problem. It was a clean shooting."

"Thanks," I said.

"It was good work."

"Sometimes the good guys win."

"One way to look at it. Now what?"

"A quick stop back at the office to get my head sorted out then home. Give my girls some daddy time then make love to my wife."

"Now that has to be the smartest goddamn thing I think I heard ya say," he said, smiling and holding out his hand which I accepted.

"Amen."

When I arrived back at the office, there were three squad cars parked out front, their red and blue flashers on the roofs spinning. I pulled to a stop and got out. There were two uniforms standing at the entrance when I got there.

"Whoa there, fella. Where do ya think you're goin'?" one of the cops said, putting his hand on my chest.

"That's okay, Pete," the other cop said. "It's Murphy. Ferguson said to let him through if he showed up. Go on in. Rodriquez is in there."

The cop dropped his hand from my chest, and I went inside, the only thought on my mind was Maggie.

A uniform cop was standing my office door. This one I recognized.

He looked over his shoulder when he saw me and called out, "Murph's here."

I stepped inside my office and took in the scene. The smell of gunpowder hung heavy in the air.

A man was laying on the floor clutching his shoulder, blood oozing between his fingers. A cop was kneeling over him. Two other men were sitting on the floor cross-legged with the hands cuffed behind their backs. One of them had an angry looking crease across his cheek from a bullet that grazed him. Blood slowly running down into his shirt.

I looked in the other direction and saw Maggie sitting at my desk, her gun sitting on top of the desk. Manny stood beside her with a hand on her shoulder. He had removed his jacket and put it over her shoulders. She looked as white as snow, obviously in a state of shock.

"Murph," Manny said, as I stepped up to the desk. "Don't worry, she's okay. Jus' shock settin' in."

"What the fuck happened?" I said, going around the other side of the desk and kneeling down next to her.

"Seems them yahoos over there came lookin' for you. From what I could get outta her, one of them pulled a gun or had a gun out, anyway she reacted by pulling a gun from her desk drawer and popped the shooter in the shoulder," he said, looking at the men on the floor. "I'm guessin' that the other one musta tried to move on her 'cause she got a shot off and jus' missed takin' his fuckin' head off. I'm guessin' that they backed off at that point and she managed to call us. That's one tough, brave girl you got here, buddy."

"Yeah," I said, putting my arm around her. "She is."

Maggie turned her head slowly toward me. I saw the light come back into her eyes as they welled up and she started to sob and shake. I pulled her head onto my shoulder.

"It's okay, baby. Go ahead, let it out. It's over."

When everyone had gone, I closed up the office and took Maggie home making sure she was okay, then drove home. I had to let Jane know what happened before she heard about it on the news and I really needed to hold my girls.

Epilogue

A month later, I was sitting in my office with Maggie and Abe. We were discussing how we were going to restructure the business since Abe was about to join us as a full partner. Before we got too deeply into this, Abe wanted a summary of the business with Gabe Herschon.

Gabe Herschon made a full recovery from his injuries. Jake Pickett, the last of the original three attackers, was arrested and arraigned on charges of aggravated assault and attempted murder. Gabe identified him as one of the men who attacked him, nearly beating him to death, and agreed to give witness at the trial. The police were able to get enough evidence to add a charge of second-degree murder for the old black man.

Jimmy Dixon packed up shop two weeks after Pickett's arrest and headed back south. As for the men who went to my office, they were still in jail awaiting trial on several charges.

Gabe sent a very personal letter to me thanking me for what I did. He also enclosed a cheque for one thousand dollars. I tried to talk him out of it but stopped when I saw how hurt he looked and thanked him instead.

Maggie said that she received a letter from Mrs. Edna Harding thanking her for what she did and to say that she has been in touch with her daughter, Caroline. They were talking and things were looking good.

I was feeling good, as I sat there with two of my friends. Maggie and Abe were laughing and getting on like a house on fire.

Looks like the gods decided that I earned a break and opened a door to a new phase in the life of Mathew Murphy.

The End

Also published by BWL Publishing Inc.

The John Robichaud Mysteries
Dead Man In The Harbour
Murder On The Docks
The Evil Men Do
The Body In Room 103
The Norwegian Woman
The Red Murders

Standalones
Unfinished Business (A Novel)

H. Paul Doucette has lived and worked in many countries throughout a varied career in International Transportation ranging from twelve years as a merchant seaman to a career as an industrial logistic specialist.

He spent a few years 'thumbing' his way across North America and Mexico during the cultural revolution of the sixties and early seventies, during which time he participated in the civil rights and antiwar movements of the time.

He has also enjoyed moderate success as a Fine Art Black and White Photographer. Now he is pursuing his interest as a writer of period set mysteries.

In addition to the Robichaud Mystery series he has also written two other series; one set in Greenwich Village in the 1960s and another war time series set in the Pacific.

He has been retired for more than twenty years and lives in Dartmouth, Nova Scotia.

www.ingramcontent.com/pod-product-compliance
Lightning Source LLC
Chambersburg PA
CBHW070010120726

47909CB00003B/863